The Tombstone Race

The Tombstone Race

Stories

José Skinner

UNIVERSITY OF NEW MEXICO PRESS • ALBUQUERQUE

© 2016 by José Skinner
All rights reserved. Published 2016
Printed in the United States of America
21 20 19 18 17 16   1 2 3 4 5 6

Library of Congress Cataloging-in-Publication Data
Skinner, José, 1956–
  [Short stories. Selections]
  The tombstone race : stories / José Skinner.
     pages ; cm
  ISBN 978-0-8263-5627-7 (pbk. : alk. paper) —
  ISBN 978-0-8263-5628-4 (electronic)
  I. Title.
  PS3569.K499A6 2016
  813'.54—dc23

                                2015017214

Cover photo: *Bernalillo Cruisin'* courtesy of Shavone Otero
Designed by Lila Sanchez
Composed in Melior LT Std 9.75/14

These stories originally appeared in the following publications:
Bilingual Review/Revista Bilingüe: "Vigil" (published as "Cop"); *Border-Senses*: "No Moo Goo" (published as "The Pedant") and "Their Songs";
Boulevard: "Clean"; *Colorado Review*: "Backing Up"; *Other Voices*:
"Crypto"; *Solstice Literary Magazine*: "The Edge" and "Looking Out";
Red Rock Review: "Judge, Your Honor, Sir"; *Third Coast*: "The Extra."

For Ly

Contents

◆

The Edge

OSVALDO AND HIS homies' favorite party spot was a place they called the Edge, on the rim of the Rio Grande Gorge. At the Edge, the flat sagebrush plain cracked and fell away to seven hundred feet of rough black basalt. The plain was like a sun-faded pool table that had split in two, and they raced their cars and trucks over it and slammed on their brakes at the last minute. Midway down the gorge hung the rusted hulk of a fifties pickup. Cans and broken beer bottles glinted on the rocks. At the bottom coiled the brown river.

Unless the moon shone, you couldn't see the river or the hulk or much of anything down there. On one of those moonless nights in the summer between Osvaldo's junior and senior years of high school, he and two carloads of his homies drove to the Edge.

They sat on the warm hoods and cracked cold beers. Every few minutes, a car or truck rumbled across the invisible bridge spanning the gorge. When they finished their beers they tossed the cans into the abyss. They listened for them to hit and, as always, heard nothing.

"Hey, eses, where's the bitches?" Leroy said.

"They didn't want to come," someone else said. "Not even Lola."

"Maybe they don't like black primer."

"Black's bad," Osvaldo said. The week before, he had stripped his Isuzu Amigo of its pinstripes and pearls and painted it completely in black primer.

"But it scares them off," said another voice.

"Maybe it's just *him* that scares them off," Leroy said, meaning Osvaldo.

Osvaldo's nickname was the Bad. Lola had given him that placa a few months before, when they were watching *The Good, the Bad, and the Ugly* at the Starlighter Drive-In. He had planned to go to the movie with Lola alone, but Leroy managed to invite himself along. That was Leroy: always getting in other people's mixes.

During the movie, the three of them had sat on the Isuzu's tailgate, Lola in the middle, Osvaldo wondering how he was going to put the make on Lola with Leroy there. When the Bad appeared on the giant screen, Lola shrieked, "That's you, Osvaldo!" Leroy laughed and said it was true. Osvaldo studied actor Lee Van Cleef's slit eyes and sharp, beak nose and high, sun-scorched cheekbones. Angel Eyes was the Bad's other name. By the end of the movie, Osvaldo had learned to shift his narrow eyes to look badass like Angel Eyes, making Lola shriek some more, driving her into Leroy's arms, who grinned and hugged her.

The Bad face was good for cruising the Taos plaza with his homies and scaring tourists. It was funny to watch a lumpy-legged couple in shorts pick up their cowlike gait after seeing his face. Mad-dogging a ranfla full of cholos was a different matter. It made his guts watery. They might cap a round between his angel eyes. But there was no other choice when his homies said, "Show them the Bad, homes." Their lives depended on him making it good, on making the cholos not want to fuck with them.

The beers got shaken on the drive over the rough road to the Edge and foamed when they were opened. Primer stained easily, and Osvaldo suspected the beer cans were making rings on the hood of his car, though he couldn't see them in the moonless dark. But it would seem joto to mention this to the others, and anyway where else were they going to put their beers? And maybe it was badass to have beer circles on the hood of your ranfla, like bullet-hole decals on your door panels.

It had rained that afternoon, and it looked like it would rain again that night. The air smelled like chemistry class. A steady growl of thunder came from the mountains, as if there were a giant dog behind them. Then came lightning, which was like God zapping the dog with a Taser to get him to shut up.

"What kind of dog would God have?" Osvaldo wondered.

"Pit bull," Leroy said.

"Listen to these locos," someone said.

"Well, I don't think it's gonna be no fucking Chihuahua," Leroy said.

A couple of voices laughed nervously at this blasphemous talk of God.

"So what kind of dog you think Satan has?" said Osvaldo.

"You should know," someone said from the darkness.

"Poodle," said Leroy, cracking everybody up.

The growling and the tasing got so mixed up that you couldn't know if the tasing was making the dog growl or if the dog was being tased for growling. As the storm approached, the growls exploded with the flashes.

People scrambled into the cars. Only Leroy stayed outside, dancing in the rain.

"Crazy loco."

"Pinche vato."

Sizzle-crack-flash, all at once, exploding around Leroy. It could easily be sizzle-crack-flash-dead-Leroy all at once too, a single event. Both cars honked their horns and flashed their lights at Leroy. But he danced away, out of the beams of the headlights.

"Somebody go grab that loco."

They said the safest place in a lightning storm was inside your car. Osvaldo never quite understood that. The tires grounding it and all that shit. Maybe people believed it just because

3

the lightning had just never *happened* to strike a car. Badass if the first car lightning decided to strike was his, right there. Badass, and fucked, too, as they all fried inside the black, electrified box.

"I'll get him," he said, forcing his door against the wind and ducking into the hail.

The others, under questioning by the police, would say that as Osvaldo approached Leroy, they saw, in the next blinding flash of lightning, horns sprout from Osvaldo's head. One boy swore he saw Osvaldo's arrowed tail lash the ground and his feet morph into cloven hooves.

Osvaldo told the police that he reached for Leroy, but that Leroy danced away, laughing, into the darkness. Osvaldo yelled, "Fuck you, homes"—a couple of the others testified they heard those words too, faintly—and scrambled back to his car. The hail had coated the ground white.

"Let's get the fuck outta here," he told the others. He shuddered with cold. The hail was nicking the new primer. If Leroy wanted a ride, he could go in the other car. Another bolt of lightning struck.

"You didn't touch him?" one of the detectives asked.

"I didn't touch him."

"So he just kind of danced out into the Rio Grande Gorge," said the detective, fluttering his fingers in the air.

"Maybe the lightning got him."

"The lightning, you think?" said the cop in a friendly tone, leaning close.

Osvaldo said nothing more. He was booked and arraigned on an open count of murder. To get released on bond, Osvaldo had to hand the title of his Isuzu over to the bondsman, and his parents had to put up the deed to their house and apple orchard.

At the grand jury hearing, the prosecutor asked the other boys what Osvaldo's demeanor was like. How was he acting?

They told about the horns and hooves. All the boys, including the ones in the other vehicle, told about it. The horns and the hooves and the pointed tail, illuminated by a flash of lightning.

The grand jury handed down a true bill. That meant, Osvaldo's lawyer told him and his parents, that he was going to trial, unless she could get the case dismissed.

"Trial? When?" said his father. On the lawyer's table, his father's hands looked as old and wrinkled as winter apples; he twisted and rubbed them together, as if trying to still their trembling.

"The date hasn't been set yet," said the lawyer, a skinny, Anglo public defender who kept brushing her hair from her face. "The prosecution is going want to continue the case—that means postpone things—until they come up with a body. Hard to get a conviction without a body. An indictment's different. As they say, most grand juries'll indict a ham sandwich."

Osvaldo's father stopped rubbing his hands and looked at her as if she were insane. His mother kept her eyes lowered.

"See, motive's all they've got at this point," said the lawyer. "Osvaldo Mondragón, aka the Bad, sought revenge for Leroy's having taken his girlfriend Lola from him. Osvaldo perceived that Leroy had made a cuckold of him, 'put the horns on him.' How does it go in Spanish?"

Now even his mother stared at her.

"Poner los cuernos, that's it!" said the lawyer. "Right? Am I right? I'm sorry, my Spanish isn't great. I'm working on it, though!" She turned pink and began to talk even faster. "The jury up here'll be mostly Hispanic, of course, and the prosecution's going to make a big thing of this horns thing, you can bet on it, and have the witnesses say they saw actual horns sprout from Osvaldo's head right before he shoved Leroy into the chasm—allegedly shoved. Exploiting people's superstition. It's racist. It's so disgusting."

"No body," said Osvaldo's father.

"I'm sorry? Oh, yes, no body. No body!"

5

Search-and-rescue teams had combed the sides of the gorge for Leroy's body, though their dogs were too terrified of losing their footing to be of much use. The sheriff's department dragged the Rio several times, fruitlessly.

"He was a floater, wasn't he?" the lawyer asked.

"Then they would have found him," said Osvaldo's father. "Floating."

"Oh, no!" said the lawyer. She gave a kind of desperate, whinnying laugh. "I meant—a throwaway kid. He didn't really have a home. Kept running away from foster care. Nobody reported him missing for three days."

"So," said the father, "he could be anywhere."

"Anywhere at all! That's right. Could've run away to Alaska for all anyone knows. That's all we need to say."

"And all my son has to say is that he didn't push him," said Osvaldo's mother. "Under witness of God."

"Oh, no! He shouldn't take the stand. He shouldn't testify."

"Why shouldn't he?"

The lawyer turned pink again. "It's better not . . . Anyway, there's no need to talk about that now. We'll cross that bridge when we come to it."

"But if he's innocent?"

"Ya déjalo, Mamá," Osvaldo murmured. He knew what the lawyer meant. After all, hadn't Osvaldo's grandmother said, when she was scolding him, that the Devil himself must have scratched those ojos rasgados into Osvaldo's face with his three-clawed hand? Hadn't an uncle once said how curious it was that Osvaldo's parents had given the boy the same name as the satanic assassin of the great John F. Kennedy? Hadn't his father called him, as a young child, "mi diablito," until it wasn't funny anymore? The lawyer was right: at the trial, he would have to sit quietly at the defense table, as far away from the jurors as possible. He could not bring his face to the witness stand to be displayed and animated before the jury, to have them see the evil yellow in those scratched eyes and the even, satanic red glow beneath his skin.

6

While out on bond, Osvaldo continued working at his summer job for the Department of Transportation, fastening netting on the slopes that rose above the highway and the river, downstream from the gorge. The DOT was eager to get the job done before the monsoon rains dislodged more rocks. Earlier that year, a boulder had loosened and bounced down the mountainside, crushing a Bible-school bus from Texas before rolling into the Rio Grande. Several children on the bus had died.

Osvaldo's fellow workers nicknamed the killer rock Baby Huey. Baby Huey was a great big clumsy comic-book baby who couldn't help breaking things and wreaking havoc. Of course, being a baby, he was innocent and didn't realize the damage he was causing. Just like the rock, which now sat guilelessly in the middle of the river, creating a pleasant swirl for river rafters to whee over.

"You don't know Baby Huey?" they asked Osvaldo. "Casper the Friendly Ghost? Hot Stuff Sizzlers?" Most of these guys were permanent employees and older than him, and those must have been old comics.

They explained. Casper was a wimpy ghost who had a ghost horse named Nightmare. Hot Stuff Sizzlers was a fat little devil with a pitchfork. All the men laughed, and so did Osvaldo. They got Osvaldo a pitchfork and had him pitch straw mulch over the newly seeded hillsides and called him Hot Stuff.

But that teasing had taken place before Osvaldo's indictment. Now the men gave him his space. Osvaldo concentrated on his work, pitching straw and moving rocks and fastening netting and thinking. Why did Baby Huey, after all those centuries of just sitting there, decide to roll down the hill at *that* moment? Well, of course Huey didn't decide anything. The rains had come, and the last molecule of dirt had released its grip, and there went Huey. And there just happened to be a church bus tooling along the highway below. Shit happened.

God's will, his mother called it. Why would God will that a church bus full of children get crushed? Osvaldo wanted to know. Just calling His angels to heaven, she said. Like Leroy, said Osvaldo. Yes, like Leroy, said his mother, looking away from him.

Osvaldo's father told him he should thank his lucky stars that Leroy had no relatives in the area to take revenge. Like if that rock had killed people with familia? The relations would have long since tied dynamite around it and blown it up, right there in the river.

Osvaldo's brothers were both in the army overseas, in Iraq. They sent him letters telling him to hang in there. Sober, formal letters, not like previous ones where they'd joked about his joining them in Iraq and scaring the enemy to death with his Bad face. They said they didn't think they could get leave to attend his trial, but that hopefully it wouldn't come to that.

The judge told him sternly to not communicate with his homies, or he'd be clapped in jail until his trial. He saw Lola once on the plaza, but she pretended not to see him and disappeared into a store. He could only hope that Lola would tell the truth, that she and Osvaldo really hadn't been going out and she wasn't his girlfriend, so how could he be jealous of Leroy?

"Don't kill yourself," one of the men murmured to him one afternoon as Osvaldo, thinking about these things, heaved straw furiously up a slope. The guy was trying to be friendly, Osvaldo supposed, break the ice a little, but what Osvaldo heard was, *Do* kill yourself.

Downriver, about half a mile from where Baby Huey sat, lived Osvaldo's chemistry teacher. Osvaldo found this out one afternoon when, over lunch, the foreman, who'd spent the morning informing people who lived downstream that the netting project would soon include the hillsides above them, told the crew about this one loco, a hippie with a bald top of the head and a ponytail. The hippie said that just because we always saw rocks roll downhill didn't mean they always would. Maybe one day they'd roll uphill; how could we be so sure they wouldn't? Had we observed the movements of all the rocks in the universe?

This loco's house was a little blue one right on the water, with weird metal sculptures all around. Osvaldo knew it had to be Gene. The dude was always saying crazy shit like that. He told the class that there was so much empty space in atoms that if you shrunk the world to where it was really solid, it would become the size of a ping-pong ball. If you got sucked into a black hole, like the one at the center of our galaxy, you'd get stretched out in a long line of atoms, feet first. Our bodies are made of so much water that you might as well think of yourself as just water doing its thing. The sun was a big hydrogen bomb, constantly turning mass into energy, and, by the way, each of your bodies has the energy equivalent in mass of thirty H-bombs, which is something you might think about whenever you're having self-esteem problems.

Gene had been a scientist in Los Alamos. No one knew exactly how he ended up being a high school teacher in Taos, but there he was, and the school was proud to have him. He had a PhD, maybe two, but he didn't like being called Dr. or even Mr., so he was just Gene. He'd once brought to class a brownish glassy thing in the shape of a lightning bolt, about half an inch thick and a couple feet long. It was melted dirt from lightning: lightning came from the ground up, he said. It occurred to Osvaldo (maybe because lately he'd been stuck at home at night watching cop shows on television) that Gene would make a great expert witness at his trial. He could bring in the glassy thing—what was it called? Fool-something—and tell the jury that since lightning came from the ground up, Leroy could have been blown sky-high. Maybe even evaporated. After all, lightning was like eight times hotter than the surface of the sun, Gene had told them.

After work that day, he told the foreman he didn't need a ride back to town; his father would be picking him up. The foreman looked relieved; since the indictment, those rides proved what Gene, quoting Einstein, said about time being relative—a minute's not the same length when you're eating chocolate ice cream as when you're sitting on a hot stove. Since the indictment, riding with the guys had felt a lot longer for all of them.

At quitting time, Osvaldo sat on a rock on the side of the road until all the crew had driven off. Then he walked down the road to his teacher's house. It was blue, all right, and perched right over the water. The sculptures were like strange windmills, their delicately balanced silver vanes in constant motion under the cottonwood trees. Gene was outside, in shorts and a Hawaiian shirt, peering at something in the water. Storm clouds billowed above the mountains to the north.

"Hey, Gene. Hey, we're working on the road, I mean, the hillsides—"

Gene shielded his eyes from the sun. "So I've been told. Osvaldo?"

"Yeah, it's me." Teachers always remembered his name. "Oh, you already know?"

"I've been apprised. You working on that?"

"Yeah. Labor."

It was always weird meeting teachers outside of school. At the movies or the grocery store or like this, in shorts. Showing up at their houses—nobody did that. He realized he'd made a mistake.

"Okay, yeah, next week we'll be up there." Osvaldo waved at the steep hillside and started back to the highway, wondering now how he was going to get home.

"Want to come in?" Gene called.

They entered the little house. Books everywhere, and two computers, a big laptop and a desktop, that looked cobbled together from all sorts of parts. Gene rummaged in a groaning old snailback refrigerator and brought out two cans of beer.

A teacher offering a student a beer! But if any teacher broke the rules, it would be Gene. It seemed pussy to tell Gene what the judge had told him, that if he broke any laws, such as underage drinking, his bond would be revoked immediately and he'd be sent to jail. Osvaldo took a seat on a tatty sofa in the dim, low-ceilinged living room. Outside, the river rushed.

Osvaldo propped his elbow on the armrest of the couch and held the beer up to partially hide his devilish face from Gene, whom he felt observing him even as he pretended to straighten the books on one of the tables.

"So how's your summer been, Osvaldo?" he asked at last.

"Not too good."

"Want to tell me about it?"

Gene listened attentively, but Osvaldo got the feeling he already knew the story. When Osvaldo broached the idea of Gene's testimony, he pointed to the glass lightning bolt on the bookshelf. "You could bring that in."

"The fulgurite?" He smiled at Osvaldo, and regarded him for a long moment. Then he asked him if he'd like to smoke a joint. "It'll help us think. Strategize."

Weed did make you think. When he smoked, Osvaldo often pondered the weird things Gene said in class.

"Like what?" Gene asked, passing him the joint.

"Like about almost everything being empty space. Like inside the atoms?"

"How about at the trial I testify to that, too? Since everything's mostly empty space, how can you say anything really touches anything? That should establish some reasonable doubt."

Osvaldo wondered if he was being serious.

"I used to work in fusion, you know. Up in Los Alamos. The hydrogen bomb: now that's really squeezing things so they touch."

"Really," said Osvaldo.

"The prosecutors could bring in a rebuttal witness and we could argue about force fields and shit." Gene giggled. "The uncertainty principle."

"The cat thing."

"Schrödinger's cat! Alive and dead at the same time."

It was getting dark. Thunder struck, and lightning flashed in the dirty window. Osvaldo wondered again how he was going to get back home.

"Lightning, man," said Gene. "Weird shit, all right. People think the lightning causes the flash. The lightning *is* the flash. No cause outside of its effects, right?"

Osvaldo nodded. Speaking of effects, this was pretty good dope. The couch felt like it was swallowing him up, but he found himself moving when Gene said, after another, louder bolt, "Come on, let's go out and watch."

They went out on the narrow, railless deck that overlooked the river. The water roiled and frothed at their feet—it was raining hard upstream. Crazy lightning split the sky. It seemed dangerous to Osvaldo to be standing out there, but he wasn't about to pussy out by saying so. Gene appeared lost in thought.

"I think," Gene said after a while, "that your best chance of winning is to dispute the motive. You say Lola wasn't your chick, right?"

"We went out a couple times."

"So no need to be jealous of her, ¿que no?" Gene was Anglo, but he thought using Spanish expressions was cool.

"Not really."

"Ever fuck her?"

This was one of those questions it was good to lie about, and the low, conspiratorial way the teacher asked it put him on alert. But Osvaldo murmured the truth, "No," and felt his face get hot.

A quavering bolt lit the mountains like a fluorescent bulb going bad. A cold breeze blew off the river. Osvaldo shivered. Gene put his arm around him.

Osvaldo didn't get touched much—his mother's hugs were always fleeting, and his father only ever shook his hand. Gene's arm felt good. But it stayed too long, solid and unyielding, and he sensed the heat of the man's thigh next to his. He waited another moment for Gene to break the spell with a comradely jostle, and then he threw the man's arm off.

"¡Pinche puto!"

"All right, now," said Gene, backing up. "What are you saying? Are you saying I touched you inappropriately? Is that what you're saying?"

The man talked too fast and too slick, as though he had been in this kind of situation before. Or maybe he just was scared. He should be scared, pinche joto, fucking with the Bad. Osvaldo took a swing at him. But either he slipped or Gene tripped him, and he fell into the thrashing river.

The river dragged him over rocks, pitched him through the froth. He cracked his head on a boulder and felt warmth on his scalp. His work boots grew heavy with water, but when he managed to get on his back, feetfirst, he was grateful for the way the boots bore the blows of the rocks as he shot downstream. Without knowing how long or how far he'd gone, he found himself twirling gently in an eddy. His buttocks scraped coarse sand and anchored him. He pulled himself onto a tiny beach on the other side of the river.

In a panic to get away from the roiling water, he clambered up the rocky slope. From the safety of the flat plain, where the three-quarter moon silvered the sage, he contemplated the river below, his scalp and elbow and tailbone throbbing. He couldn't make out Gene's house, and it was impossible to tell how far the river had carried him. Fucking Gene! But with his mind now cleared by the shock of the water, he wondered if the dope hadn't made him paranoid back there, hadn't exaggerated the length of time the man had had his arm around him.

The closest place he knew of for crossing back to the other side of the river was the bridge over the gorge, several miles— exactly how many, he had no idea—to the north. All he had to do was walk over the rocky ground between the clumps of chamisa and sage and grama grass, keeping the river on his right until he got there. He set out, his soaked boots squeaking. After a few steps he caught a glimpse of a flashlight beam sweeping over the water below, and he heard Gene's voice calling him, a hoarse, pleading voice: "Hey. Hey, Osvaldo. Hey, man."

He walked on. The storm had receded over the mountains and the wind had died down, but he was still cold. He stopped and took off his clothes and wrung them out. For a while he walked only in his boots and his underwear, so the damp clothes wouldn't chafe his skin. The chasm to the river deepened.

Several hours along, when the moon was high and small, he lay on his side to rest. He couldn't lie on his back, because his tailbone, which must have struck a rock in the river, hurt more than ever. The wound on his head had swollen and become tender all around. So things don't really touch things, Gene, you stupid fuck? Maybe Gene could tell the jury that other thing he'd said in class, that just because you saw something happen the same way a million times didn't mean it would happen that same way on the million and first. You just have faith that it will. One day a rock might run up a hill instead of down. Maybe Leroy had flown into the sky instead of fallen into the gorge. Why not? Everybody now seemed to think Leroy was an angel anyway.

He shivered his way into a fitful sleep. He dreamed he was falling headfirst into a chasm, and when he hit bottom he hit just so, causing the atoms to fuse into a nuclear explosion. He opened his eyes to the first rays of the morning sun blasting into his face.

No more than half a mile farther along, his body stiff and his clothes still damp and his stomach an empty hole, and there it was, the steel lace of the gorge bridge, bright in the early morning sun.

A single car, a beige hatchback of some sort, was parked in the viewing area, someone sitting on the hood. As he got closer, he saw it was a girl with short, glossy black hair, writing in a notebook. From what he could tell, she was alone. The car had California license plates.

Absorbed though she appeared to be in her writing, she sensed him. She slipped the notebook under the black jacket next to her and watched him calmly. Her lip rings glittered in the sun. She couldn't have been much older than he was, maybe twenty. Dressed all in black. The upper end of a red-and-black tattoo crawled from under her T-shirt and up her neck.

"What's up?" he said.

She didn't draw back at his approach, and no fear clouded her sunlit eyes. A tough Goth chick.

She shrugged. "Sun's up."

"Feels good."

"To you, especially. You're wet."

Osvaldo offered no explanation.

"You hungry?" Without waiting for an answer, she reached under the jacket and produced a foil-wrapped burrito. He took it. Chorizo and egg, the picante already in it, warming him from the inside as the sun warmed him on the outside. Perfumed steam rose from the sagebrush. The gorge lay deep in morning shadow, the river a black snake.

He eyed the corner of her notebook and wondered what the writing was about. He couldn't help but think of the several people who had jumped from the bridge in recent years. The last guy, who'd driven up from Santa Fe, had brought his sack lunch with him and written the good-bye note on the bag. Before that, a couple had jumped, holding hands as they sailed into the abyss—their hands the last thing they touched before hitting bottom.

"They're looking for you, dude," she said.

"Who? Where?"

"Down on the highway, by the río? Search and rescue big time. Divers and the whole shebang. Don't tell me that's not you."

He waited a while before answering. "Yeah, that's probably me. My chemistry teacher pushed me."

"Your chemistry teacher pushed you. Okay."

"Or I fell. I probably just fell. It's complicated."

"Always."

He told the story from the beginning as best he could, his brain foggy from lack of sleep, his eyes fixed on the pink-and-blue smudge at the Edge where people had placed plastic flowers to mark the spot of Leroy's disappearance. Miles beyond stood the dark mountains that birthed the lightning storms.

"Well, if you're gonna skip bond, this would sure be the time to do it," she said.

"What do you mean?"

"Because in about two days you're going to be presumed dead. Unless somebody sees you. Here, get down."

He crouched in front of the car. A truck went by, making the bridge tremble. The car's license plate in front of his face read California, plain and simple. When the trembling stopped, she said, "Coast is clear." He found himself gripping the chrome fenders of the car; but as she touched his hand, the lightest of touches, his grip loosened, and he rose.

Looking Out

IF JENNIFER TOLD the story of her life so far, would she tell it as a beautiful dream, or as a nightmare? That's what Rufino asked her, up on Lookout Mountain. It was a beautiful question. No, it was more than that. It was *sublime*.

"Honey, your life *is* a beautiful dream," said her mother, holding both Jennifer's hands in her own. "But even beautiful dreams sometimes have bad parts in them. That's just reality."

Jennifer's mother wanted Jennifer to tell what happened between her and Rufino on the mountain as a nightmare. She wanted her to tell it that way to Headmaster Paxton and even the police.

Jennifer pulled her hands out of her mother's and jumped from the couch. "Maybe my life's a nightmare and Rufino is the only beautiful part!" She stumbled to her room and threw herself on her bed.

Her mother didn't even know him! No one did. He sat in the back of the class, like all the unknowables, and never said anything. A big, freckled rock, trapped behind the leaf of his desk. There were rumors about his having done time in the juvenile jail, the D-Home or whatever they called it, but like all good rumors, she didn't know where she'd heard this. He lived south of town, where his family raised horses and alfalfa or something. He had big farm-boy hands, full of blood.

Headmaster Paxton and the other administrators must have known at least something about him, because this was a private school and they didn't let just anyone in. Rufino was good for the school's diversity, they knew that much. He called himself a Chicano, but he could probably mark four or five boxes on one of those what-race-do-you-belong-to questionnaires. His freckled skin combined oddly with his kinky black hair. Small brown eyes and a broad nose. Big teeth. He really wasn't very good looking. But then neither was she, was she? He sat at his desk, silent, one of his heavy, green-veined hands dangling at his side while the other cupped his chin.

He'd been admitted that fall. In late September some jocks from one of the public high schools had crashed the homecoming party and tried to start a fight. That was sport for them, picking on the prep school wussies. Rufino waded into them, slopping his big fists into their faces as girls screamed in terrified delight. People thought that would be the end of Rufino at Prep, but in fact Mr. Paxton congratulated him. Let townie bullies be warned! Still, the incident hadn't won him any friends at the school. People were even more afraid of him now.

Jennifer and Rufino had English class together. At the time of Rufino's proposal to her to go up to Lookout Mountain with him, they were studying Romanticism. To Jennifer, *romantic* had always meant walks on the beach and candlelight dinners with someone you loved, but their teacher, a small, dark-haired woman with a smile full of secrets, liked to point out the dark side of the Romantic writers. Even Blake's *Songs of Innocence* were full of ominous moments, such as the shadows and darkening at the end of the "The Echoing Green"; and "The Blossom," though it only talked about birds in trees, was about how you can be sexually attracted and repulsed by the same person. The sparrow in the poem, she added, was a phallic symbol. The important thing about Blake, she said, ignoring the snickers, was the way he kept two conflicting things going at once and then took them to another level.

Then there was this Romantic thing called the sublime,

which Jennifer understood was something like when you looked out at the desert or ocean from a mountaintop and felt afraid but not really, because even though you knew that all that out there was a lot bigger than you and could swallow you up and you were nothing in comparison and were mortal, you were still *you* and alive to tell about it.

At study period, she looked up the word "sublime" in the index of a library psychology book. The entry was followed by "subliminal," "submission," and, a little farther down, "suicide." She noticed the way the book's cover dented the bright blue veins of her wrist, and she slammed it shut. The sound was practically sublime itself, an echoing boom in the library that made heads look up, including Rufino's, who turned his strange face slowly to hers.

She left the library and went down into the arroyo behind the gym and lit a cigarette. At home she also had to hide in an arroyo out back to smoke, because her mother hated, absolutely hated, smoking. That was fine for her mother, who was skinny as a stick and didn't need to lose weight; but Jennifer did, and smoking helped.

Rufino followed her. He scuffed the ground and asked her what she thought of their English class.

She took a drag, exhaled through her nose, and said, "It's sublime."

He scuffed.

"I'm joking," she said.

"I know." He swung his freckled face up and looked worriedly at the mountains. Jennifer followed his gaze.

"It really is sublime from up there, I guess," she said (somebody had to make conversation). "The view."

"Yeah," he said. Then, "Wanna go?"

"Up *there*? Like, *now*?"

"No, I don't mean now."

"Well, when?" She couldn't believe she was helping him ask her out, but she was.

"Tomorrow."

"Tomorrow's a school day."

"Yeah," he said.

She was afraid that if she didn't say yes he might not talk to her again.

"Maybe," she said at last.

"What's maybe mean?"

"Maybe means maybe."

His face turned red, the freckles disappearing in the flush. "But what does it *mean*? What's maybe *mean*?"

"*Okay*," she said. He was like a child, but a really intelligent one. "Tomorrow, then."

Her mother called it Lookout Mountain because she could never remember the real name for it, Atalaya, which meant the same thing, but in Spanish. (Until she was probably eight years old, Jennifer thought it was Look Out Mountain, like in "Watch out! You're going to fall.") Though Jennifer had lived in Santa Fe since she was little, she hardly ever went hiking in the mountains. She didn't like heights; she had a lot of falling nightmares. Falling to your death seemed so absurd, yet it was the simplest way to die. First I'm up there, all alive; then I'm down here, like totally dead.

She'd never really noticed the rocks at the top of Lookout Mountain until that day in the arroyo. It was hard to tell how big they were. Houses, she supposed. There was one particularly big, craggy one at the very top. Anyone standing on it would be too tiny to be seen from town. It was weird to think that once you had been up there, forevermore you could look at it from any point in the city and say: "I was up there."

The morning of her and Rufino's hike, she got up early and sneaked into the kitchen and made a cheese sandwich. She took her books out of her backpack and replaced them with the sandwich, along with a pint of Evian water and a rain poncho. Oh, yes, sunscreen on her face. She burned easily. Her complexion was what her mother called milky, a description Jennifer found repulsive.

She bicycled past the school. Probably people saw her from

the classroom windows. Well, fine. Rufino was waiting for her at the trailhead, as agreed, his heavy arm dangling out the window of his mud-spattered pickup.

Rufino dragged his pack off the front seat of his truck and shrugged it onto his back. He slammed the door, making bits of manure in the bed of the pickup tremble. Jennifer locked her bike to the signpost, which read, "Atalaya 2.5 miles."

The mountain loomed before them. She could see the individual trees on the rim, serrated against the sky. The boulders up there looked precarious. She wanted a cigarette badly, but it wasn't right to begin a hike with a smoke.

Rufino went first, shrugging his backpack some more to get it comfortable. He had a shambling gait, like a bear's.

"Rufino," she said.

"Yeah."

"Are there bears up here?"

It took him a while to answer. "Sometimes, I guess."

"Did you hear about the two guys walking in the woods?"

"No."

"They came across this bear. A grizzly. With cubs. The first guys goes, 'What do we do?' The second guy goes, 'Run.' The first guy goes, 'Are you kidding? You can't outrun a bear.' The second guy goes, 'No. All I have to do is outrun you.'"

"That's a good one."

In fact, it was kind of horrible, like all jokes. That's what made them funny, being kind of horrible.

The first part of the trail ran fairly flat, the chamisa bushes oily smelling in the sun, but they soon began to climb into the shadows of tall trees. Rufino forged ahead, his breathing heavy.

"I have to stop," Jennifer said. She was out of breath too.

Rufino's face was flushed, his hair sweat-matted to his forehead. Even his small eyes looked hot. He let his pack drop from his big shoulders and took out his water and drank big gulps. Jennifer drank her own water and then lit a cigarette. Okay, so cigarettes were anti-nature, but she had to have one.

They had come to a bend in the trail that showed, between

the trees, the city below. Behind the city stretched a range of mountains like a long blue cat.

"That's school," he said.

"Where?"

He pointed to flat roofs dotted with silver bells.

"Maybe we should go back," Jennifer said.

"You said that?" her mother said. "You told him you should go back?"

"I said 'maybe,' Mother. *Maybe* we should go back."

"And what did he say?"

"He said it hadn't gotten sublime yet."

"What was *that* supposed to mean?"

Jennifer began to cry then. She suddenly felt great pity for her mother. The only thing she'd ever heard her mother call sublime were the éclairs from the Chocolate Maven.

Her mother held her head and stroked her hair and waited for her to continue.

Jennifer snubbed the cigarette out against a rock very carefully so it wouldn't start a forest fire (she didn't tell her mother about the cigarette; she had to be very careful about what she *did* tell her) and gave a last glance at the school before she and Rufino continued up the trail. Inside one of those buildings their classmates were gathering for English class, vaguely aware that a couple of losers were missing. Assholes: they'd already forgotten that Rufino had saved them from those high school thugs. And little did they know that she and Rufino were about to experience what they were only studying.

The only person they saw on the trail was a woman coming in the opposite direction with a walking stick and a muscular Rottweiler on a leash, which she pulled up short as they passed. The dog was probably bigger than a wolf, but it wasn't sublime. A dog could never be sublime like a wolf, a wild thing. Were there wolves up in these mountains? She didn't think so. In any case, wolves didn't attack humans, or so she'd learned in school. Now, snakes . . . Were snakes sublime, or were they just gross? Actually, she really didn't even find them gross. One time when she was little she woke to find her stepfather standing over her only in his shirt, a stiff snake peeking out through the shirttails. As soon as her eyes fluttered open he disappeared. He disappeared so quickly and silently that she couldn't be sure it wasn't a dream. That's what her mother would probably tell her—it's only a bad dream, go back to sleep—so that's what she told herself, though she didn't think it was a particularly bad dream, just strange. She remembered it the next day, and at breakfast she told them about it. "A snake, huh?" her stepfather said in that fake voice he always used with her, but even more exaggerated now, almost a shriek. "I felt sorry for you," she said. And she added, gaily, "I always do!" Her mother barked a sudden laugh and he broke into a weird grin and turned red. Later her mother prodded her for more information about this dream, but Jennifer didn't have much more to say about it. Soon afterward the stepfather left the home, and her mother didn't marry again. After that it was just her and her mother and her little sister, in houses without males; even their cats were all girls. Her mother moved them from what she called "nasty old Chicago" to the fairy-tale town of Santa Fe and enrolled the girls in private schools, where she believed they'd be safe. It wasn't until later that they found out that Santa Fe had one of the state's highest rates of reported rape.

Jennifer and Rufino climbed. The air thinned and cooled. Her head grew light. Every now and then a break in the trees offered a view of the approaching mountain, which looked strangely close and faraway at the same time, like the dreamworld backgrounds of medieval paintings.

Then she found herself ahead of him, and she wondered how that had happened. The trail became much steeper as they neared the top of the mountain. They had to grab the jutting trailside rock to keep their balance. Small chunks of white quartz rolled under their feet. One of the authors they were studying who wrote about the sublime also had a lot to say about what things were beautiful and what things weren't.

He'd probably say the color of the quartz was beautiful, but not its jagged shape. Only smooth, rounded things were beautiful. Her milky legs, for example.

Her self-consciousness tripped up her gait and she slipped on the mica-slick rock and fell forward. She pushed herself up before he could help her. Her scraped knee glittered with specks of mica even after she brushed it off, and a few tiny droplets of blood welled and joined the silver sparkles.

Finally they reached the saddle of the mountain. Sweat trickled between her breasts and dampened her bra. She drank what was left of her water and was still thirsty. Rufino offered her his, or rather, the extra water he carried in his knapsack.

"Wait a minute, wait a *minute*," said her mother. "He had another water?"

"In his pack—"

"Was it fresh? Was it sealed?"

"What are you talking about, Mother!"

"Listen to me, Jennifer. Was it sealed? You know, sealed? Did it go crack when you opened it? You know, snap, crackle, you know *cra-ack*, like that?"

Had her mother lost it? And then Jennifer got it. Her mother thought maybe he'd spiked the water with—what did they call them?—roofies or something.

"My God, Mother, I don't know! Yes! It crackled."

God, why was she telling her anything! A nightmare, this was a nightmare!

The top of the mountain was strangely parklike, with short grass between the trees and rocks, and the trees looking as if they had been pruned and tended, except for a lightning-shattered one split right down the middle, leaving the yellow heartwood jagged and bright.

"Need to make a pit stop," said Rufino, and he lumbered off behind a boulder.

She needed to pee too. Funny how even when you're thirsty you have to pee. She went behind a tree on the other side of the trail. She looked down at the padded crotch of her panties. Her period was starting; she was just beginning to spot.

Speaking of spots, what was that? She flinched from the thing crawling near her foot, and then saw it was just a ladybug. She let it crawl up her finger. Round, cute little thing. It flew off. Ladybug, ladybug, fly away home, your house is on fire, your children are gone. Who would invent such a horrible nursery rhyme? Why were children's minds poisoned with such things?

She rejoined Rufino on the trail, which continued along the saddle of the mountain for a while. To her left, between the trees, she caught glimpses of the vast, golden desert spreading out to where the earth actually seemed to curve. It made her queasy.

"There's a rock up ahead where you can see it all," Rufino said.

"I don't think I want to go there yet. I feel a little dizzy."

"You felt dizzy?" asked her mother. "Like you were going to faint?"

"I was *hungry*, Mother!"

"Do you want to eat our lunches now?" Rufino asked.

"Yes."

They sat in the shade of a grove of pines and ate their lunches. Rufino had brought a bean burrito and a boiled potato. She offered him a bite of her pimento cheese. He'd never had pimento cheese before. He declared it good stuff. He offered her more of his water.

"You mean, he kept the water for you? When he gave it to you the first time, you gave it back and he kept it for you?"

"Yes!" She knew what her mother was implying: that he could have slipped something into it when she wasn't looking. Rufino and his roofies. Oh, hideous, Mother!

"I felt fine, Mother, fine!" In fact, she did feel a little better, after her sandwich, but still light-headed. A smell of decay rose from the soil—was it a good smell, or a bad? The spot where they sat was like a pasture with tasseled grasses and

25

blue flowers—what was the word? *Pastoral.* On the right it fell off into dark ravines and to their left were the boulders, the ones you could see from the city, beetling out into the sky. Her knee still sparkled, though the specks of blood were dried black now. She tried to wake herself with a cigarette, but even after smoking she began to nod, overwhelmed by a dreamy fatigue. Not drugged! Just sleepy . . . a nap . . . But she wasn't sure she wanted to nap in front of him, and anyway, he wouldn't let her. He wanted to get to the rock and show her the sublime view.

They clambered up one rock and down another, she following him, and headed to the farthest boulder, which jutted into the void. And suddenly they were there, suspended in space, tilted into the sky, the tawny desert stretching out to distant mountain ranges, the adobe city below a mere insect-like disturbance of the earth. The only signs of life were the occasional knife-like glints slicing up from some distant windshield or window. Directly below rose the pointed trees, like green-cellophaned toothpicks.

This silence would swallow up her scream like a puff of vapor. But she didn't have the breath to scream. She had to stay perfectly still and keep her balance and look straight ahead. She mustn't let it overwhelm her, yet she had to submit to it. She had to bring it into her, make it a part of her. . . .

His voice startled her. "Jennifer."

"What."

"Something I was wondering."

"What."

"If you woke up from your life, would you tell it as a beautiful dream, or as a nightmare?"

He was somewhere behind her, a little to the left, but she was afraid to turn around and face him.

"He was behind you?" said her mother. "And you were afraid?"

"How do you wake up from life?" she asked Rufino.

"Like maybe . . . when you die?"

26

Why was he talking like this? But she knew what he meant. She knew exactly what he meant, though she had never thought about it that way before.

"How about you?"

"How about me what?"

"Is your life a beautiful dream, or a nightmare?"

"I could tell it either way."

"So how do you tell it?"

"Depends on who I'm telling it to."

"So how do you tell it to yourself?"

"Depends."

"On what?"

"On what part of me's listening."

"And how do you know what part of you is listening?"

"That depends on how I tell the story."

Mother: "I'm sure *that's* true. He'll tell his version whatever way it helps him get out of this."

She wasn't understanding the conversation at all, her mother. She was just hearing what *she* wanted to hear.

"Rufino. Grab me."

"*Grab* you? You told him to *grab* you?"

"Catch me, I don't know, Mother! *Hold* me."

Her mother held her for a long while. Then, still holding Jennifer's hands, she looked into Jennifer's eyes and said, "What happened then?"

"Nothing!" Jennifer looked away. She could feel her mother's eyes boring into the side of her head.

"Nothing? What does 'nothing' mean? What does it mean, Jenny?"

Jennifer didn't answer, and her mother sighed one of her forever sighs. She told Jennifer to rest and that she'd be back soon.

Jennifer sat up in the bed. "Where are you going?"

"Just to the drugstore."

"That's all? Just to the drugstore? Then you'll be back?"

"Yes," said her mother, wearily. "I'll be right back."

27

Jennifer fell back on her pillows and listened to her mother drive away. She knew what her mother was getting: the morning-after pill. Okay, whatever. As long as she didn't call the cops, like she'd threatened to earlier. God, she was so tired. Too tired to go to the arroyo for a smoke. Too tired even to cry anymore. Almost too tired to think about Rufino, his big hands grabbing her . . .

Tomorrow—the morning after. That's when she'd wake up to her nightmare life, or her beautiful one.

Clean

◆

IT'S ALL IN the wrist, they told him. Otherwise you're going to
get mottles and blots. And the body men would take the spray
gun from him and show off their master control of speed and
angling, toeing and heeling and fanning, their perfect 50 percent overlap on each pass. You'll learn, they said.

Instead, Eddy quit. He could do better for himself and his
girl than be an assistant paint tech in Rey's body shop. He
went home and lay on the bed and smoked while his girl got
ready for work. The place opened before him like a stage set
of exactly what it was, a tenement apartment in Albuquerque's Southeast Heights. Ripped Naugahyde sofa spilling yellow guts, chipped lip of a fiberglass bathtub, a brick-revealing
gash in the plaster wall. A smeared window showed hardtail
choppers and tuna-boat cars in the dusty parking lot like
vague, cutout props. Only the TV picture, now that he'd rigged
up a black box for tapping cable, shone bright and clear, glittering with life and laughter. Shiny, happy little black and
white and brown kids in bright clothes, Kmart kids teasing
and tossing each other on a satin sofa, in front of their own
console TV.

"I got this great idea," he told his girl as she leaned toward
the bathroom mirror and dotted her face with makeup. "What
if you had this show where the TVs in the show were tuned to

the other shows actually showing at that time? That would give it a leg up, because then people would see that this was the real show, and those others were just TV."

The girl worked the makeup into her face with upward strokes of her fingers.

"It's a great idea," he said. "It's just a matter of selling it to the right people. It's called intellectual property."

"What if it backfires, Eddy?" she said. "What if it just reminds people that those other shows are on, and they switch?"

She possessed a certain amount of negativity. She also had god-awful zits. Now that he was clean and off dope, he noticed things like this a lot more.

"Slather that shit on," he said about the makeup. "It's all in the wrist."

She stepped into her baggy, black busboy pants and tucked in her white blouse. Her tits were something else. Bad zits, great tits. She went down to check the mail. The concrete steps trembled as she went down and trembled as she came back up. She brought the electric bill and the usual assortment of catalogs and plopped them on the bed. Then she left for work.

He lit a fresh cigarette and leafed through the catalogs. J. Crew sucked, all that casual earth-tone shit. Johnston & Murphy was more like it. They offered a spiffy Ralph Lauren chaps blazer and paisley silk ties in brilliant jewel tones. The Aristocraft mocs in smooth burgundy veal would go excellently with the blazer. He ordered by phone, using her credit-card number. Then he leafed through the Frederick's of Hollywood and ordered a catsuit for her. He got so busy he almost forgot his appointment with his PO at Drug Court.

The first time he'd gone to the courthouse—for his arraignment—he'd gone high. The bailiff made him take his dark glasses off and the judge looked into his pinprick pupils and ordered a urinalysis. The test cup showed positive and the judge revoked his bond. He later copped a plea to the possession charge and was sentenced to the Drug Court program.

Today the lighting in the courthouse men's room didn't seem as blurry as when he'd gone in that first time, because now he was straight. The probation officer looked closely as Eddy filled the test cup. The PO had to; guys were known to strap a sample of clean urine to their leg and squirt it into the cup through a fake dick.

"Last time a guy watched my dick like that in a men's room he got his head flushed," Eddy told his probation officer.

The PO didn't seem to think that was funny. They left the restroom, the cup warm in Eddy's hand.

"Ever feel like you're in a movie?" said Eddy. "Like everything you say is just a line? 'Last time a guy watched my dick like that he got his head flushed.' Sounds like a movie line, don't it?"

"You don't know when to quit, do you?" said the PO.

The PO was a middle-aged man with a pink, wrinkled face. An old puppet too many children had mooshed. He had a shit job, watching guys piss into cups all day, and he knew it. Eddy felt like saying, *At least I knew when to quit my own shit job.* But he didn't say that, because he didn't want to piss off the old piss tester, and because one of the requirements of Drug Court was to keep full-time employment.

"I quit dope, anyway. I'm clean."

When the blue line appeared on the cup, the PO said, "I guess you are."

When Eddy was first getting straight, his bones had hurt. He had become intensely aware of them, of how he was built of their pain. He could still feel their porousness where the poisons had leaked out, and an itching in the marrow. But his blood felt strong now, his joints lubricated. And he didn't play with his blood anymore, like he had at first. He no longer sat on the bed and pulled it into an empty syringe and slammed it home, over and over like that.

And attending Drug Court wasn't so bad. Even stars were sometimes sentenced to Drug Court: Robert Downey Jr. and Tom Sizemore, for instance.

"I think I'm going to make it," he told the PO. "I got this feeling."

"I'm glad you feel that way, Eddy," said the PO.

The clothes he'd ordered for him and his girl arrived by UPS in three days. He showed them to her.

"The ties match your face," Eddy said. "Polka dots."

"Fuck you, Eddy." She began to cry.

"Hey, it's just a joke. Come on, try on the catsuit. Nobody said you don't have a great bod. Hell, you've got a model's bod. You've got the bones."

She modeled the catsuit and they fucked. He told her he loved her. Then he told her about some new acne drug he'd seen on TV, Retin-A or something like that.

"Retin-A?"

"Fuckin-A."

She didn't laugh, but that was all right. She needed to get serious about her zits. Because her zits were the only thing holding them back now. He was clean; now she needed to be. Beauty might be only skin deep, but that was just it, it was only skin deep.

She dressed for work. Eddy went into the bathroom. He wiped away a constellation of spatterings from the mirror and turned on the sun lamp and got out his shaving things. He had a handsome face. A few months ago it had been the face of a handsome guy down on his luck; now it was the face of a handsome actor playing a guy down on his luck. That's how he liked to think of it.

He wondered if his girl ever used the lamp, as he had suggested she do. It probably just freaked her out. That ultraviolet light really made the skin look bad. It showed every flaw. But ultraviolet was good for more than skin, or so he'd heard. It made vitamin D, and vitamin D was good for the bones. That was a funny thing, how light was good for the bones.

The lamp went out with a metallic ping. As he took a piss of good, clean, substance-free piss, he opened the door to tell her that the lamp was good for the bones, but she'd already left.

"I went to the dermatologist, Eddy," she said a few days later. She showed him the brochure from the dermatologist. It wasn't called Retin-A, it was called Accutane. Good God. The girl in the before-treatment picture really had acne bad. A lot worse than his girl. She was completely cured in the after picture. A miracle.

"It costs, though," said his girl.

"How much?"

"A thousand. It costs a thousand, Eddy. That's just for the pills."

"One large? What pills cost one large?" He'd heard Jimmy Cagney say "one large" in an old gangster movie and liked it.

"Well, they have to do a lot of checkups. They have to take your blood. That's part of it. You take the pills for four months, and they take your blood every month. To make sure you're not pregnant."

"Pregnant? What does pregnant have to do with it?"

"Birth defects, Eddy."

"Shit. You're not getting pregnant. Tell them you're not getting pregnant."

They'd already had the baby talk. He didn't want them. Even now that he was clean, he didn't want babies. He let her cry. It was okay to cry. Crying got rid of emotional toxins.

"That's not the way they do it, Eddy," she said. "They won't give you the pills until you get the blood tested. It's scientific. Hey, Eddy? The pills could hurt my bones way later. They don't know yet."

"Bones?"

"Years from now. They don't really know. It's experimental."

"Like a guinea pig thing? Well, well. So a thou for the pills. Then what?"

"Then there's the collagen shots for the scars. And the derma-something. What does it say here? The dermabrasion. It's like real fine sandpaper. They sand my face, Eddy."

"How much is that? The sanding and the shots."

"A few thousand, depending. Maybe they can do it with laser, he said. They'll see after the pills. First you have to take all the pills."

"Can you put it on your card? Doctors take plastic, don't they?"

"I've reached my credit limit already, Eddy," she said.

"Well, no biggie," said Eddy. "Rey'll lend me it. Of course, if I can't pay him back later? He'll-a break-a my legs."

"Then we'll both have bad bones," she said.

Rey ran a chop shop. Not too many people at his legitimate body shop knew this, but Eddy did. The chop shop was in a garage off an alley, behind steel curtains. An explosion of parts lay on the concrete floor. Rey's chop people could strip a car in nine minutes.

"Hey, it's the paint meister," said Rey. "Come to help us paint some panels."

"Nah," said Eddy. He glanced at the door panels on the floor. They were where Rey stashed the cash they took down to Mexico to be laundered.

Eddy told Rey he needed a loan.

"How much?"

"Just a large. One large."

"What's that? Large."

"A thousand."

"One large," said Rey, and laughed. "What's the large for, steady Eddy? Got a deal on some shit?"

"No, I'm clean. It's to fix up this little beaut I've got."

"Little beaut." Rey liked to repeat the things Eddy said. Rey had thick-looking yellow-brown skin. Eddy thought maybe he was some kind of Indian.

"Chevelle?" Rey asked.

"'Vette. '67 'Vette."

"Tight little number. Bring her in, let's take a look at her."

"Nah," said Eddy, and Rey laughed again.

Rey took a stack of bills and placed them in a money-counting machine next to a greasy crankshaft. The machine whirred and counted. Rey handed the stack to Eddy.

"Everything's counted and accounted for around here, Eddy," said Rey. "Very scientific. You like science, Eddy?"

"You bet," said Eddy.

Eddy's girl got the pills. A month later her face was worse. Her lips were cracked and her breath stank. The skin on the soles of her feet peeled and smelled bad when she came back from work.

"The doctor said things would get worse before they got better," she said. Her eyes glistened.

"That's the way it always is, isn't it?" he said. "I should know." He'd gotten tired of her crying. She cried a lot more now than when he'd been strung out, and that wasn't right. As if she was happier when he was weak, when he didn't notice things like her zits, or didn't care. When he had been strung out, she'd hardly ever cried. She'd helped him get straight, helped him when his bones hurt, and now he was trying to help her, that's all.

"Listen, Eddy, I got an idea. So you won't have to look at me or be with me till I'm well? I'll go to my mom's in LA. Then the next time you see me I'll be fixed. I'll get the surgery done there. They've got great plastic surgeons in LA."

"Maybe that's good," said Eddy. "Maybe that's a good idea. I'll join you when you're well. LA's the place for us. LA's the place for beautiful people, and you'll be perfect."

"And then maybe you won't like me. If I was perfect, you wouldn't want me. Because now you always have to have something to bitch about."

For the first couple of weeks, she called Eddy every day. She said her skin was still bad, but the only thing to do was wait to see if the pills would work.

After a while she was only calling every three or four days. But she said she was getting better, and she sounded good. She said she was already lining up a Hollywood plastic surgeon for the collagen shots and the dermabrasion.

"Hey, that's great," said Eddy. "Hollywood's got the best plastic surgeons. Well, hallelujah. Didn't I always say with good skin you could be an actress or a model? The sky's the limit for us, babe."

"But, Eddy? It costs, Eddy. The plastic surgery."

"So you borrow it from your mom."

"She doesn't have it, Eddy."

That was a lie, but Eddy let it go. "Okay, I'll talk to my people again. No problemo. Once you're fixed we'll be making it and we can pay them back. I can feel it in my bones. Hey, babe? I can't wait to see you."

"Don't come yet, Eddy," she said. "Let me get it all done first. I want to be perfect for you, Eddy."

Eddy assured her he'd send her the money.

In October, soon after he sent the money, the calls stopped. Eddy got in touch with her mother. Her mother sounded hard. She said his girl was no longer living there and that she didn't know where she was.

"Call again or come around here, Sport, and I'll have a restraining order slapped on you so fast it'll make your head go gaga," she said.

Sport. She sounded like a tough old broad in a Cagney movie. Eddy thought they could get to like each other, if she'd give him a chance.

Eddy considered trying to reach his girl by calling all the Hollywood plastic surgeons. But he knew Hollywood plastic surgeons would protect their patients' identities like pit bulls.

Eddy asked his PO, "You guys ever take the blood?"

"Sometimes," the PO said. "Would you rather give a blood sample? It's more precise."

"Measures all the poisons."

"That's right."

"Nah."

The big mistake these people made was thinking that the

dope was the poison that caused the rot. But the rot came way before the dope. Eddy's mother knew. After punishing him, Eddy's mother used to tell him, looking evenly into the face that refused to cry, "Rotten to the core." Sometimes she'd add, "Born rotten." Eddy's girl knew too, now.

"Where's the blood made?" Eddy asked the PO as he handed him the warm cup of urine.

"In the marrow, I think."

"Yeah, that's what I thought."

The blue minus sign appeared on the cup again. Still clean.

"People don't think about their marrow," Eddy said. "They think about their heart or their brain or their skin. But when do they think about their marrow?"

The PO regarded him tiredly with his old doll's face.

"But what's deeper in you?" said Eddy. "What's more inside of you? What's more the core of you?"

"You be good, Eddy," said the PO.

Eddy went to Rey's chop shop to get his punishment.

"What you mean, you can't pay the tab?" said Rey. "Sell the beaut."

"That's just it. She's gone."

"Gone how?"

"Jacked."

"Jacked? We'll kick their ass."

"It happened in LA."

Rey told Eddy to come back the next day and start painting panels. Then they kicked Eddy's ass. Eddy took his beating in silence, on the floor, curled into himself to protect his core.

The new Frederick's of Hollywood catalog was waiting for him in his mailbox. He hobbled up the stairs and tossed it on the bed. He turned on the sun lamp and examined his cuts in the mirror. There was a deep one under his chin but the rest seemed shallow enough. He dabbed his face with cologne. He hoped the deep one wouldn't scar.

He placed the cologne on the shelf that held her apricot

masque and her oatmeal face pack and her Kiss My Face honey-calendula and olive-aloe moisturizers. When the sun lamp pinged out, he swept all her things into the trash.

He took his rig from the floor of the closet and tied off. He slapped a vein to life and sunk the empty needle into his arm. Dark blood swirled into the syringe and he slammed it home. He did this over and over, until he relaxed.

He put the works back in the closet and lit a cigarette and leafed through the catalog. It showed lots of girls in catsuits and lace. None of them were his girl. He closed the catalog and lit a cigarette and gazed at the sculpted shag carpet. The pile of the shag rose high, but not high enough to hide ancient scorch marks. He flicked the butt into the rug and watched it go out.

If you get some runs in the clear coat, don't worry about it, they told him. Better to sand out a run and reshoot the panel than have the whole job orange peel. If you get the quarter-moons, clean out the gun's air-horn passages. If teardrops show, check to see if your needle's not clogged. You'll catch on, they said.

Crypto

I MET MICHAEL Goldblatt for the first time in Spanish 103, Elementary Spanish Conversation. It was the first day of class, January 22, the day following Martin Luther King Day. We were going around the circle, introducing ourselves. This was after the professor, an impish old man from Spain who'd been teaching at the University of New Mexico forever, gave us a little lecture on "to meet" versus the Spanish "conocer." In Spanish, you meet someone once and thereafter you simply encounter one another, he told us. In English, you meet someone, and before you take your leave you might plan to "meet" again; in English, he marveled, you're always knowing someone as if for the first time!

"Another thing," he said with a mischievous smile, "'introducir' and 'to introduce' are false friends. In Spanish, you only want to introduce yourself to already good friends. Remember, there are diseases out there. In Spanish, you *present* yourself to someone you don't know." He began with me. "Usted, ¿cómo se llama?"

I was nineteen years old and easily embarrassed. I was embarrassed to be in Spanish 103 in the first place; as a Chicano, I should have been in Spanish for Native Speakers, but that was too advanced for me. And, of course, I was embarrassed at the old professor's humor. Now I found myself recalling from my

Intro to Anthro class that female apes, when they wish to copulate, and males, when they want to show submission, turn and "present" their rears to dominant males.

Blood pulsed in my neck. "Emeterio Benavídez," I croaked, looking at the floor. My old-fashioned given name—it had been my grandfather's—mortified me.

A voice came from my left. "Benavídez, from Ben-David, son of David. Emeterio from emet, Hebrew for 'truth.'"

That the words were said in English when we were supposed to be speaking Spanish gave them a certain urgency. I looked over and beheld a lopsided grin beneath a massive, majestic nose, a nose like that of the Great Sphinx before Napoleon blew it away. A gimlet light shone in his green eyes.

"Couldn't help it," he said. "I've been studying names."

"¿Y usted quién es?" asked the professor. "¡En español, hombre!"

"Michael, um, ¿Miguel? Goldblatt. Nombre judío. ¿Cómo se dice 'gold leaf' en español?"

"Oro en hojas. ¿Su nombre significa oro en hojas?"

"Sí. Goldblatt, oro en hojas."

Goldblatt explained in halting Spanish how the Jews of Europe had been forced to choose European surnames in the nineteenth century. Names like Goldblatt, meaning gold leaf, were known as "ornamental" names. I didn't think I'd ever heard a name as ugly as Goldblatt. But its Spanish translation, "oro en hojas," was beautiful. A technique I had developed to distract myself from self-consciousness was to repeat a beautiful phrase over and over in my mind like a mantra, and now I did this with "oro en hojas," running the three words together as one, like the professor did: oroenhojas, oroenhojas.

After class, Michael Goldblatt came up to me in the hall and said, "I didn't mean to out you back there."

Anxiety welled in me anew. "Do what?"

"You're a Jew, too. I'm sure of it. A name like Emeterio Benavídez? A crypto-Jew, a secret Jew, a converso. You know—a marrano!"

No, I didn't know. To me, marrano meant "pig." There were standard barrio responses to something like this. Most simply: Fuck off, joto. But I wasn't very good at macho aggression. Besides, his directness disarmed me.

"No, really, you should look into it. Ask your parents."

My parents? He was a know-it-all, but he didn't know my parents.

"My parents are Catholics," I said.

"Sure they are. So are their parents and their parents' parents. All conversos are, since the time of the Inquisition. Jews had to convert to Catholicism or else."

I shrugged.

"Well, I could be wrong," he said. "Wouldn't be the first time. Where's your family home? Here in Albuquerque? You still live there? Yeah? I'll come over to your place sometime and we'll look for clues. There's always clues."

The thought of Michael Goldblatt coming over to my house and looking for clues to my family's supposed Jewishness made me nervous. My parents, as I'd told him, were good Catholics, particularly my mother, who went to mass regularly and was active in our parish. My father seldom went to church, but in a way his Catholicism was more rigid, because it was more cultural than spiritual. No questioning of dogma or crises of faith for him; if the Pope said X was the way it had to be, well then X it was, because we were hispanos, and therefore Catholics. My father also had a habit of making anti-Jewish remarks when he was hungry. He'd be watching the television news, waiting for my mother to serve supper, and he'd start in on the Jews, and the blacks, and the Anglos too. After stuffing himself he was okay with all of them.

My sister Bernice presented another problem: she would flirt with Michael. And after he left, she would roll her eyes and sigh, "Your friend's a fox!" I knew my sister. I knew her taste from the days I used to loll on her bed and look at movie-star magazines with her. She didn't like the pretty boys; she wanted them strong-featured and masculine, like Michael. She was twenty, a year older than I, living at home again after a brief and bad marriage, working at Whataburger and waiting for a new guy to come along. I didn't want Michael to be that guy.

But my misgivings made no difference. Michael Goldblatt was going to come over and declare us Jews, my sister was going to declare him a fox, and I felt powerless to stop any of it. Not only could I not stop him, I made it easier for him by waiting for him after class the following week.

"Well?" he said. "Found any indications?"

"Of what?"

"'Of what?,' he asks. Of the big secret."

"I don't know what to look for."

We walked down the hall and out of the old Pueblo-style adobe building.

"So you want me to come over now?" he asked.

"Now?"

"Aren't you curious?" Then, with a little irony in his tone, "And don't you believe what it says up here?" He pointed to the long, square-cut viga above the portal. In timeworn, hand-carved letters, it said, "And the truth shall set you free." I'd never noticed it before.

He poked me on the chest. "Emet, truth. Remember? And the emet shall set Emet free."

We went in his car. I didn't have a car; I took the city bus to school. His car was an old black Audi, its roof and hood faded by the New Mexico sun. Heat had cracked the dashboard but the beige leather seats felt supple and good.

"Don't get started about a Jew driving a German car. I didn't buy it new, all right?"

"I didn't say anything."

"These cars got a bum rap. People were swearing they were accelerating on their own. Consumer groups did a thousand tests on them. The conclusion? Drivers were hitting the accelerator instead of the brake. The pedals are a tiny bit closer together than on other cars. People refused to believe that, though. They prefer to believe in ghosts. Their capacity for self-deception is infinite."

He eased us onto Central Avenue. The late afternoon sun, warm through the windshield, struck the tops of his thighs, lifting an aroma of new denim. This mingled with the scent of the old leather, and I felt enveloped in a bubble of warm and confident masculinity. I wanted to keep going west, on and on, to California, where I'd never been but which stood for me somehow as the symbol of freedom.

We lived in the old barrio of Los Griegos, near the Rio Grande. Michael said, "That's a last name, Griego, right? Means 'Greek'? So tell me: How did Chicanos become known as Greeks? Or was it Greeks who became Chicanos?"

"I'm not sure," I said.

"I'm here to tell you," he said. "Everybody's all mixed up."

Our house was a low-ceilinged clapboard, painted green. My grandfather had built it. He, and his father before him, had farmed the acreage behind. But the formation of the Middle Rio Grande Conservancy District and the rising property taxes that followed had forced my grandfather to sell the farmland off. Later my father sold the water rights to a land developer, the proceeds from which, he made sure to let me know, were the source of my tuition and book money. My father now worked for the District, driving around all day in a pickup, checking on the flow and drainage of the remaining irrigation acequias. He resented the "outsiders" who had urbanized Albuquerque: the Anglo lawyers and bankers, the Italian and Jewish merchants. He dreamed of some pastoral past when homelessness, drugs, gangs, sexual perversions, and other "big city problems" supposedly did not exist.

Michael inspected the doorframe as I unlocked the door. "No mezuzah," he said. I had no idea what he was talking about; later he would explain to me that the mezuzah was a little container attached to the doorframe in which scriptural passages were placed, and that it had evolved from Passover, when God told the Israelites to sprinkle lambs' blood on their doorposts as a sign to Him to pass over their homes and not kill their firstborn.

My father, fortunately, was still at work, and so was Bernice. My mother, I knew, was in her room, taking her siesta. I didn't want to wake her, so I hurried Michael down the hall to my room. He had to duck down the length of it—my grandparents had been small people.

He glanced around my bedroom, hunting, I supposed, for further "clues." His gaze landed briefly on my teddy bear in its rocking chair. I'd had it for so long, all my life in fact, that neither my family nor I noticed it anymore. But now I could hear this stranger thinking, *A nineteen-year-old guy with a teddy bear?*

He opened my closet door and inspected my coats, his long, olive fingers caressing the lapels until he found the labels.

"Looking for shatnez," he said.

"For what?"

"The mixing of linen and wool. It's against our law." The hangers squeaked as he slid them along the rod. "So far, so good. Yep, looks like you're clean."

"But I never pay attention to what clothes are made of. I just get what I like."

"Well, the avoidance is probably instinctual by now," he said. "So many generations of it. Okay, now on to the food. No, wait, first: Do you have any, like, totally empty rooms in this house?"

"Empty rooms? No. Well, there's this little room in the basement—"

"Sort of hidden, right? Show it to me."

Yes, it was hidden, and empty. So hidden and forgotten that when I wanted to masturbate in the daytime I would sneak down there to do it. I had no lock on my bedroom door, and knocking was only perfunctory in our household. The bathroom door had a lock, but the hidden room was more exciting than the bathroom; its hiddenness, its secretiveness, aroused me. Now I was going to show this secret sanctum to my new

44

friend. My testicles tightened as I led him down the rickety basement steps, around the boiler, and to a narrow, hand-hewn door. We creaked the door open. Feeble light glowed in the dirty ground-level window. You could barely see anything, save for the very emptiness of it, but the circular stains I had left on the concrete floor, coins of sin I'd never been able to completely lift, jumped out at me.

"This is a hidden prayer room. Your grandfather built it?"

"I guess." *A hidden prayer room!* Which I had defiled for years. "But nobody prays here."

"Of course not. Typically crypto—the reason why's been lost, but the tradition of building them goes on. Now, where's your kitchen?"

My mother was not keen on strangers in her kitchen, but I led him there anyway.

He rummaged through the freezer first. "Excellent. No shellfish."

"We don't really like shellfish."

"Exactly."

"It seems weird to us, I guess because we're so far from the ocean—"

"Na, na, na, don't give me that. It's because you eat kosher. Aha!"—he was in our refrigerator now—"the milk and the meat are on different shelves. I'm beginning to discern a definite pattern."

My mother appeared silently in her slippers. With eyes still confounded by sleep, she stared at this stranger crouched in front of her refrigerator, shoving things around in there.

"¿Qué buscan?" she said.

"Mami? This is Michael."

Michael stood, head and shoulders taller than she. "Hi. What's your maiden name?"

My mother looked at me beseechingly.

"It's Silva," I murmured.

"Silva! Not to be confused with Silver, but still Jewish. Sephardic." He smiled his lopsided smile.

45

"Michael's into history," I told my mother. "But we gotta go now."

Michael forged ahead. "To escape the Inquisition, the Benavídezes and Silvas and Rubíns and all the other Spanish Jews—I can give you the whole list—had to convert to Christianity or get burned at the stake. So who can blame you? Meanwhile, you kept certain secret customs. A prayer room. Separating the meat from the milk. Let me ask: Do you always bathe on Fridays, then dress in clean clothes?"

"Michael's Jewish, Mami," I said, finally.

When I was a child, my mother had placed a sign in our front window that read, "No religious solicitation. This is a Catholic household. Please respect our faith." She'd put it there to discourage Jehovah's Witnesses and Mormon missionaries, but those people weren't easily discouraged. In fact, the sign seemed to entice them, draw them in to what was sure to be a stimulating theological wrangle with someone as dogmatic as they. It also encouraged homeless people and winos to come to our door, hopeful of the charity the sign seemed to advertise.

Despite its ineffectiveness, the sign stayed for years, and I remembered it now, because I remembered my mother's expression the time a particularly devious proselytizer wormed her way into our living room. When the woman began to talk about the Pentecost, my mother's lip curled and her eyes narrowed, her normally soft features sharpening to a look of disgust that I'll never forget. She was looking at Michael in that same way now.

"Oh, I'm Jewish, all right," said Michael, smiling again, seemingly oblivious. "Are you kidding, with this schnoz? What's interesting is that you are too, quite possibly."

A car crunched on the gravel outside. "Bernice is here!" I cried, as if my sister didn't come home every day at this time from her job at Whataburger. If at first I'd been reluctant to have her meet Michael, her appearance now was a godsend. I hustled Michael to the living room and opened the door for her.

She was still in her tight uniform and smelled of grease and fries.

"Bernice, Michael; Michael, Bernice," I said. "So! How's work, Bernie?"

Bernice batted her eyes at Michael and lifted her bust provocatively as she took off her coat. I could hear my mother rummaging around in the refrigerator, trying to figure out what this judío, this Jew, had done to our food.

"Gabriella got busted again making out in the parking lot with her boyfriend on company time," said Bernice. "She knows she's gonna get fired, so she's giving away free stuff all next shift."

"Hey, I'm hungry, let's go," I said to Michael, pulling on his sleeve.

We were quiet on the way downtown to the Whataburger the city would soon tear down to make room for the new Metro courthouse. The sun was sinking, and Michael's car was cold now. I wondered if he was thinking about the look my mother had given him. I didn't know how to apologize for it.

The intercom at the Whataburger drive-through squawked for our order.

"Is Gabriella there?" Michael said.

"This is her."

"You know why Jews have big noses?"

"What?"

"Do you know why Jews have big noses?"

"WHAT? Come around to the window, I can't hear you."

We drove up to the window. Fat Gabriella stood there, looking half-pissed.

"You know why Jews have big noses?"

"No, why?"

"Because the air's free."

"Hi, Gaby," I said, leaning over. I could smell Michael's faint body odor.

"Whatchu guys want?" she said, looking really pissed now.

"Free," Michael said. "What's for free?"

"Everything's free," Gaby said. "Whatchu want?"

We ate our free burgers and fries and shakes in the Whataburger parking lot, watching, through the dusty windshield, the January sunset darken from mauve to gray. The food warmed my stomach and gave me new confidence. I kept glancing at Michael's profile, at that powerful, well-built nose. I liked it. A nose that knows it's a nose, on a Jew who knows he's a Jew.

"Why do you make those jokes about your nose?"

"The same way blacks call themselves niggers or you Chicanos joke about all the beans you eat."

I'd never heard a Chicano joke about beans, but I didn't say so.

"You know what they're thinking, so you confirm it," he said. "You recuperate the power of your degradation."

Michael drove me home. My father's pickup was in the driveway; he was back from work and no doubt hungry. He and Bernice were peering out the front window when I walked in the house.

"That the guy?" my father said.

"He's a cutie," Bernice said.

"I don't care what he is. He upset your mother. He tells her she's a Jew. What's up with that? What kind of friends you making at school, hijo? He don't come back to this house no more. ¿Entiendes?"

I made a face at my father's back and winked at my sister.

I believed Michael when he said we were Jews, and it thrilled me to have him as the friend who had discovered the secret. We began to meet frequently after class to get something to eat. Michael had been reading newspaper reports—he loved reading the local papers, and he always had the latest *Weekly Alibi* in his car—about the E. Coli bacteria found in various fast-food joints, so he didn't want to return to Whataburger, which suited me fine because my sister worked the afternoon shift and I didn't want her flirting with him.

The bacteria had even been found in the iced tea at the

Golden Corral, Michael said. The name Golden Corral made Michael laugh. "Sounds like an S&M club," he said.

I had no idea what he was talking about.

"But you do know what the Earl of Coli's main residence is, don't you?" he said.

"Not really."

"The White Castle!"

"I don't get it." White Castles were some sort of East Coast fast-food chain; we didn't have them in New Mexico.

"Ah, Emet. There's so much you don't get."

We went to Bagelmania ("If a seagull flies over the sea, what flies over the bay?"), where he explained to me that true bagels were boiled to produce the hard, shiny skin.

"But don't get too excited about Jewish food in general," he said. "Pickled fish. Dough soaked in chicken fat. Yuk."

"But aren't you supposed to eat all that?"

"Oh, I think you mean kosher, are you supposed to eat kosher. No, not necessarily. I don't."

This relieved me, because I knew pork was not kosher, and my family ate pork like it was going out of style: pork tamales, pork carnitas, pigs' feet in the beans.

Michael explained to me that there were a million different kinds of Jews—observant and unobservant, Orthodox, ultra-Orthodox, secular, self-hating . . .

"Self-hating?"

"Jews that wish they weren't Jews. But you can't really fault an individual for not wanting to be an involuntary member of some group, can you? A member of a group that those not belonging to have voted you a member of."

"No," I said, uncertainly.

"Because who decides who's a Jew? It's not always the Jew who decides."

"But he can hide. . . ."

"Like you cryptos did for four hundred years."

"Not anymore," I said.

He grinned his toothy grin. "Nope, not anymore, buddy."

One crisp but sunny February day, I suggested we go hiking in the foothills east of the city. Michael had transferred to our university from a school in New Jersey, his home state, but despite his having been in Albuquerque six months already, he had yet to explore the mountains. If he didn't want to walk, we could sit in the car and watch the sun set over the Navajo Nation and talk about things Jewish.

A shiny, black pickup truck was ahead of us as we traveled up Indian School Road. It had an inverted pink triangle on its bumper.

"The Nazis made them wear those triangles, just like they made Jews wear the Star of David," Michael said.

"Who?"

"The gays."

"Oh."

"Hitler couldn't get them all, though. There were secret homosexuals in the highest ranks of the SS."

"Cryptos." I blurted it without thinking, and felt my face get hot.

"That's right! Crypto-queers."

I knew "queer" was one of those derogatory terms that had been "recuperated," as Michael would put it, by the gays. You could even take classes in Queer Studies at the university. But I couldn't tell whether Michael's use of the word was derogatory of gays or meant to show solidarity with them.

We turned in to the parking area at the trailhead. "Whoa," said Michael as the city below came into view.

"It's even better from those rocks," I said.

"You want to hike way up there?"

"It's not that far."

I led him up the trail. It wound around boulders big as houses; they had tumbled down the slope as if kicked from the summit by a giant in a tantrum. The silence was as gigantic as the landscape.

The trail grew steep, and I became aware that my ass was at Michael's eye level. I wondered how he saw it, and I wondered why I was wondering this, and my self-consciousness grew so acute I felt I had to stop or fall forward on my face.

"What?" said Michael.

"Nothing."

"You hear something?"

"No. You want to go first?"

"Me? No. Why?"

"No, nothing. I was just asking."

"You go ahead."

Michael had mentioned newspaper reports about the bears and mountain lions wandering into Albuquerque from the high country that lean winter. I didn't think they had such creatures in New Jersey, and I supposed, with an odd combination of disappointment and relief, that he was more concerned about encountering such a beast than he was about the movement of my ass.

The wind grew sharper and colder as we climbed. We got to a jumble of boulders that formed secret nooks and cubbies, still warm from the day's sun. In one of the crannies, fawn sand had gathered into a soft bed; I recognized it as a place where I'd once masturbated.

"Any snakes down there, you think?" Michael said.

"I doubt it," I said. "Do you want to go down?" As soon as I said it my throat dried like the sand below.

Michael babbled as we descended. "Jesus, if we get bit . . . Look out for their skins, that's a clue. I was at this place in Jersey, friend of a friend's place. I saw in the bathroom trash what I was sure was some kind of condom. Real thin, kind of scaly, some expensive, exotic kind. A long tube of it. I thought, *Christ, the guy's hung like a horse.* Then I found out he had a pet python, and that was its shed skin."

We reached the bottom of the crevice. It was like descending into a kiva, those stone-walled rooms where Indian men went to conduct their secret ceremonies.

I saw where my bare toes had dug orgasmically into the sand on my last visit here, and I felt a weakness in my limbs.

Michael looked around for signs of snake and, satisfied there were none, sat beside me.

We were silent for a moment. I followed his gaze to the profoundly blue circle of sky above us, which held a single faint, unblinking star.

"Speaking of shed skins," he said quietly, "are you circumcised?"

My heart clenched. Why was he asking me that here, in this secret, hidden place? Was he making a pass at me? A cool, menthol sensation flowed in my blood.

"You know what circumcised is, don't you?" he said.

"Yeah," I whispered.

"So are you or aren't you?"

I knew Jews were supposed to be circumcised, but my father wasn't, and he was proud of the fact that, when I was born, he had resisted the gringo doctors' strong recommendation that I be. Sometimes, when he was waiting for his dinner and watching television news about the Middle East, he'd say: "Los judíos me la pelan, y los árabes tambien." The Jews can peel me, and the Arabs too. He'd say it out of earshot of females, because it meant: I invite the Jews and the Arabs to roll down the foreskin of my uncircumcised Chicano Catholic dick.

"It doesn't matter," Michael said when I didn't answer. He got up, brushed off the seat of his pants. "If you're not, it's just proof of your people's need to hide your Jewishness, right? Because if a clipped dick means getting burned at the stake, forget it, right? Ready to go back, Emet?"

On the hike back to the car, Michael told me the joke about the rabbi who collected foreskins. "Those foreskins, what are you going to do with them all, Rabbi?" the other rabbis asked. "You'll see," he says. Finally one day he shows them this little wallet he's made. "That's it?" they said. "After all that work?" "Yeah," said the rabbi. "But rub it, and it turns into a suitcase."

I laughed. This, I thought, must be what they meant by Jewish humor, this ability to laugh at yourself, your religion. It had been a confusing afternoon. I didn't know how to interpret a lot of things that had been said or the things I had felt. Michael was right, there was a lot I didn't know and didn't "get." But I knew one thing: it was great to be a Jew.

One day, our Spanish teacher brought up for discussion the controversial new downtown statue of the Spanish conquistador Juan de Oñate, who had colonized vast stretches of New Mexico, but who had also cut off the feet of the rebellious Indians of Acoma Pueblo. Someone, perhaps a Native American, had recently sawed off one of the statue's feet in the middle of the night.

Eventually the discussion touched on another controversial piece of public sculpture, the Holocaust memorial soon to be unveiled in Civic Plaza. The memorial was a fifteen-foot black metal chimney made of swirling human figures—people going up in smoke. Among its detractors was a group of Holocaust survivors living in Albuquerque. A girl in our class agreed that it was in poor taste.

I glanced at Michael to see what he thought of this remark. I was expecting him to say something angry, or at least sarcastic, like, "Yes, it's very bad taste to burn up six million people." But he kept a conspicuous silence. Afterward, in the car, I asked him why he hadn't said anything.

"So why didn't you?" he retorted. "You're not a Jew?"

I said nothing.

"Actually," he said, "I'm against the memorial myself."

"Why?"

"Tired of the passive victim thing. You know, before World War II, Jews had a reputation for being a tough people. We weren't easily fucked. Now we're thought of as the people who were led like sheep to slaughter."

"What about the crypto-Jews? We weren't passive victims?"

"Definitely not. You're survivors. You did what you had to do. Did you know Oñate himself was one? It's well documented."

"Oñate? But he cut off those Indian guys' feet!"

"Yeah, he did. Hey, I'm not saying he was a great guy. But he was one tough motherfucking Jew."

As always now when Michael drove me home, I didn't ask him in. He seemed to understand why, though I'd never mentioned how upset he'd made my mother, or my father's banishment of him.

I found my father ensconced in his recliner, watching TV news and waiting for his dinner. The TV showed Palestinian children throwing rocks at Israelis, and the Israelis shooting back.

"Quihúbole, Dad."

"Mijo," he murmured, without looking at me.

I watched for a minute, then announced: "Oñate was a converso."

"What's that, hijo?" The name Oñate had gotten his attention. My father was a fierce supporter of the statue and outraged that someone had hacked off its foot.

"Juan de Oñate. A Jew who converted."

"You're still with that? Still hanging out with that guy?"

"A tough Jew. It's well documented."

My father snorted. "Los judíos me la pelan. The Jews are de los otros."

"Los otros?"

He made his wrist go limp and his voice falsetto. "You know. Del otro bando." Then he intoned, "Be careful, hijo."

De los otros. Del otro bando. Those others. The ones on the other side. These were barrio terms for queers. What if—I was careful to make the question hypothetical—you were de los otros? How would you locate your kind? If you were bold, what they called "out," you might attend one of those meetings for queers on campus. If you were of drinking age, and could work up the nerve, you could go to one of those scary-looking bars like the Mineshaft. If you weren't squeamish at all, you might answer one of those Men Seeking Men ads in the back of the *Weekly Alibi* in which some stranger described in lurid detail the things he wanted to do with you.

Or you might sit in a toilet stall in the remotest restroom of your classroom building, telling yourself you're there to poop but in fact just staring at the message carved on the wooden door, "suck me here, 2:00," wondering how fresh the carving is (it looks fresh, the wood splintered and blond), wondering if these kinds of messages are legit or cranks, glancing at your watch, not because you're anxious to know how close it is to 2:00 (no, of course not, it's because Spanish class is at 2:30 and you don't want to be late). 1:59 now.

You hear the door creak open. This is an old bathroom, with frosted glass in the door and a transom above it. The partitions between the stalls reach almost to the floor, so you can't see the shoes that whisper across its yellow tiles. You listen to the unzipping, the splashing. You hold your breath, but why are you trying to keep quiet? You exhale, and the next breath you take catches, midway, in a kind of sob that makes you wince. The splashing stops. You listen to a listening, and again, out of instinct, you hold your breath. The urinal is flushed. You tell yourself to breathe normally. Water runs in the sink, a towel is yanked, hands are dried. The feet give a couple of steps—back, you believe. What's he doing? Examining himself in the mirror? Reading the graffiti on the door of the stall next to yours? Gradually you lower your head to see if you can see his feet, and you glimpse the side of a white sneaker with black stripes. Your blood rushing in your ears, you ever so gingerly clear your throat, a querulous clearing ending on a high note. You wince again: it's so plain to you that it's your own voice. The spell, if there has been a spell beyond your imagination, is broken. The feet whisper away, the frosted door slams.

You yank up your pants, slip out of the restroom, get lost among the students in the halls. A few minutes later you're in class. You can't help but stare at Michael's sneakers. They're white with black stripes, but two other boys wear identical ones. Everybody wears sneakers. Conversation and wholesome laughter bubble around you. You hear your teacher's voice through a fog: "Emeterio, ¡ponga atención! ¿Qué le pasa a este chico? ¡Estará enamorado!"

People laugh. You look up, and they stop when they see how fiercely you are blushing. As soon as class is over, you bolt.

That night, Michael phoned. My sister answered.

"The fox," she whispered to me.

I took the call in my room. Michael didn't mention my embarrassment in class, as though he hadn't noticed it, and got right to the point: "Listen, man, do you think you'll be up to going to the memorial dedication on Sunday?"

"What memorial?"

"The Holocaust memorial."

"I thought you were against it."

"That's not the point. The point is, it's happening, whether we like it or not. We should show some solidarity."

"Yeah, sure. Of course I'll go."

The rest of that week, I burned. Better to beat off than to burn, I told myself, paraphrasing St. Paul, and twice I went down to the empty room off the basement. But each time, I turned around and left before I unzipped my pants. That was a prayer room, and I would not defile it.

I refused to do it at night, too. I would not give in to lust. Lust was what had driven me into that toilet stall. Lust was a deadly sin, and it was one los otros were all too good at. Because of it, they had their own holocaust, called AIDS.

Love was something else. Love was the supreme virtue. "Estará enamorado," the Spanish professor had said. "He must be in love." He was right. True, I'd crouched in a filthy toilet stall, burning with lust, and that was shameful. But I knew what love was too, I did.

I wasn't sure how many more times I was going to be able to see Michael, after Sunday. The school term was coming to an end, and apparently he wasn't going to stay in Albuquerque for the summer. We'd gone around the circle in class and said what we planned to do over the summer, and Michael said he'd probably have to go back to New Jersey where he knew he could get a job that paid better than New Mexico's poverty wages. It was the first I'd heard of those plans. When my turn came to tell of my own plans, I said, stupidly, "No sé." I had imagined doing a lot of things with Michael—hiking, exploring the Mexican flea market, soaking in the hot springs, going to the genealogical library and searching for crypto-Jewish names. But what was I going to do alone? No sabía. I didn't know. Pine. Burn.

When Michael came to pick me up that Sunday, he waited in his car, like a date your parents don't approve of.

"I'm not really sure if I want to go to this thing after all," he said as we drove down 2nd Street. It was a warm, sunny May day, a fine day. Michael wore a gray silk short-sleeve shirt. Clean, tight jeans. I trembled.

"That grotesque chimney with those swirling, crying figures," he continued. "Some drama group is putting on a piece called 'Cattle Cars.' The Jews are forever the people loaded onto cattle cars and led passively to their deaths. Like fucking cows. Jesus!"

He chewed his lip as we drove into the dim coolness of the underground garage beneath Civic Plaza.

"We don't have to go," I said softly as he pulled into a space.

"No, we don't," he agreed. He turned off the engine and the lights. A door slammed at the end of the row and footsteps echoed away from us. The garage grew quiet.

"So what do you want to do?"

"I don't know. What do you want to do?"

Then I took a deep breath and said, "I don't want to be passive anymore."

"What do you mean?"

I'd like to think that what I did then contained no element of lust, that it was a gesture of pure comfort, of love. I'd like to think I had some sensitivity to the moment, and I tell myself that had I been able to see, in that darkness, the distress on his face, I would have seen how awful my timing was, how inappropriate, how consumed I was by my own desire, and it would have been like a handful of sand thrown onto my burning. But I didn't see his pain in full until the lights of an incoming car lit us up, and by then I already had my hand on his thigh.

He looked down at my hand; and in the brief moment before the other car turned off its lights and threw us into darkness again, I saw his eyes narrow and his features gather into a look of contempt very much like the expression on my mother's face when she'd learned he was a Jew. Oh, so he's one of those. One of them. De los otros.

"Wow," he said. My hand shot back into my lap, where I pinched it hard with the other.

My voice cracked. "Wow?"

"I never . . . Wow."

I bolted from the car and ran up the garage stairs and into the brightness of the plaza. People were gathering around the veiled memorial. Jews. More Jews than I'd ever seen in one place.

I hurried across the street and into the Hyatt hotel. I took the escalator to the mezzanine and peered out the windows. I saw Michael glancing around the crowd. I backed away and fell into a plush purple chair, melted into it with shame and self-loathing.

After a while I became aware of a man in an identical chair, watching me. He was an ugly man, a very ugly man—uglier than the Jews who spat on Jesus, as my mother might have said. His fat bulged into his suit, baldness shone between the strips of long greasy hair laid over his skull, he had a double chin and a porcine nose and tiny eyes too close together. When he saw I was regarding him, those eyes shifted a little, but not so far that they couldn't hold me in their periphery.

I felt a cold heat in my limbs. I got up, wandered to where he could see me better. I leaned my arms on the golden railing of the mezzanine and gazed down at the lobby, sticking my ass out a little. Then I went into the men's room.

The ugly man was not long in following. He stood at the urinal next to mine. He unzipped but made no splash.

He cleared his throat. "I've got a room here," he said, a quaver in his voice.

The menthol power flowed in my blood.

We left the restroom together. We stood in silence by the elevator. He looked straight ahead at the brushed aluminum doors, as if regarding me would break the spell of his good fortune and I would disappear like a genie.

His room looked out on Civic Plaza. I sat in a chair by the window and gazed out while he hung his coat in the closet.

The Holocaust memorial had been unveiled. A man with a rabbi's long beard and black hat was giving a talk from the podium, but the words were inaudible through the sealed window. Off to the side, a group of high school girls in black were rehearsing a dramatic piece—"Cattle Cars," I imagined. I couldn't find Michael in the crowd.

The ugly man came up behind me, touched my hair tentatively, my neck. His belt was undone: I could feel its buckle dangling at my spine.

"What's down there, young friend?"

"Just a bunch of Jews."

I turned to him. "I hate Jews. You're not a Jew, are you?"

He stared at me, astonished. He took a step back, his hand clutching his buckle.

"If you don't want to do this—"

I tried a smile. I could see it in the mirror above the bed, a ghastly version of Michael's lopsided, winning grin.

I stayed with the ugly man for many hours, a plaything for him, a toy. He offered me money to stay until morning, but around midnight I walked my exhausted, sore body home. My mother, preferring unconsciousness over worry, had taken a pill and gone to bed, but my father was waiting up for me, as was my sister.

"Where the hell you been, hijo? What's with this not calling or anything?"

I drew in a breath, but it caught in my chest, and I was afraid to answer lest I begin to weep.

"I know you weren't with that Jew guy, because he called a couple of hours ago for you. He sounded worried."

"He's a fag," I murmured.

"¡Ay, no!" my sister said.

"True, hijo?" said my father. "Did he try anything?"

I hung my head.

"¡Lo mato!" my father shouted.

"No, Papi. It's okay. I jumped out of the car. It was a long walk, is all."

"Jumped?! Are you hurt?"

"No. Just tired."

My father slammed his fist into his palm. "¡Sinvergüenza! They got no shame. No shame. That cabrón."

I didn't know if he meant Jews or fags had no shame. Both, I guess.

I went to bed, and I slept most of the next day. I don't know whether Michael ever tried calling back; if so, nobody gave me the message. I never called him, and I skipped our last class so I wouldn't have to encounter him. I never saw him again. And we never mentioned him again at home, either. We never spoke about our Jewishness, or about what he'd done or tried to do to me in his car that night, for shameful things are best hidden, even if they can't be forgotten.

The Tombstone Race

THIS THAT I'M about to tell happened in the Vietnam Era, before the Village People and their parody of the macho man, and before the general public became aware that bars for tough guys weren't necessarily bars for tough guys at all. Billy's Bar was a tough-guy bar, or so everybody in town thought. It was named in honor of Billy the Kid, whose nearby grave is our area's biggest, or should I say only, tourist attraction.

A life-size cutout of the Kid with his Winchester at his side, his pistol grips backward the way he liked them, his baggy pantaloons making him look wide in the hip and narrow in the shoulder, his head nearly swallowed up by his sugarloaf sombrero, greeted you as you swung through the saloon-style doors of the bar. This plywood cutout was fashioned after the famous tintype of the Kid, which was then the only known photograph of him.

Life-size was surprisingly small. The Kid was a little guy. Dare I say it? Girlish, even. A blowup of the tintype hung behind the bar. A tintype shows an image in reverse, as if in a mirror, so you're actually looking at an inverted Billy the Kid in that iconic picture. It's hard to tell from the portrait if he's wearing what his killer, Sheriff Pat Garrett, rather lovingly described, in his memoirs, as "a neat boot to his small, shapely foot."

61

Elmo Nolan was the owner of Billy's. Elmo, in contrast to Billy the Kid, was a very big man. He had light-blue eyes and shiny red cheeks and a fluffy, straw-colored beard. The light from his eyes seemed to glance right off his cheeks when he laughed. People attributed to his presence and personality—and to his size—the fact that things never seemed to get out of hand at Billy's, despite the alleged brutishness of its customers.

Elmo, who was single, had worked for years in the West Texas oil fields, roughnecking and tool pushing, and with the money he saved he opened Billy's. He'd had it for not quite six months. The building, a couple of miles southeast of town, had previously housed his parents' café, and for a long while after they died it sat there with the stucco falling off and Russian thistle growing on the roof and the Chinese elms cracking the foundation until Elmo rode into town on his shiny new Harley to rescue the place. Everybody was glad that this native son had come back, because so few did; and nobody minded that he opened a bar for motorcycle people as long as he kept things under control, which so far he had.

Those were still the days when "men were men," at least in our part of the world. If a boy from our town was called to serve his country, he went. When my older brother Alex got his Selective Service draft notice in the summer of his nineteenth birthday, he knew what he had to do.

Alex didn't have an opinion on Vietnam. That is, he shared the general opinion of folks in our area, which was that war wasn't a matter of opinion. The most they might say about this war was that it was a matter of preserving the nation's honor. Everybody by then knew that the US was going to pull out of Vietnam without actually winning the war. But the pullout had to be gradual, in a way that would "save face," as President Nixon said, even if a few more boys had to die in the process.

Alex did have a definite opinion about the GI uniforms. The day after he got his notice we sat side-by-side in one of the yellow Formica booths of our parents' Circle K convenience store and leafed through *Uniforms of the World*, which was one of the picture books we kept next to the road atlases and which never sold, and he wondered who on earth had come up with those baggy, drab-green pants, clunky boots, and netted helmets. Whatever happened to the plumed busbies of the hussars, to high-top kepis and peaked shakos? Handsome helmets like those fawn-colored Zulu-war ones with their silver-sphinxed plates? What became of braids and frogging? To the Red Barons, with their leather jackets and rakish scarves and goggles perched jauntily on their heads? No wonder the American soldiers wore such hangdog expressions on the nightly footage from Vietnam.

"Camouflage," I said. "Isn't the green for camouflage?"

"So smart," he said. "For a *girl*."

"And you have so much fashion taste—for a *boy*."

I scrambled, but he pulled me back into the booth, got his arm around my chest, and pounded the back of my head till I saw brightness. I could smell the foreign fragrance of the French moustache wax he used to darken the sparse hairs on his upper lip. I squirmed away and got to safety behind the corn-dog warmer, my breasts searing from the struggle.

"And why do they have to shave our heads?" he said, running his hand through his sandy cowlick. "It makes everybody look the same."

It's to erase your individual identity, I could have replied, had I been that smart. And to make it easier to catch you, if you desert.

My mother—though not my reticent father—told people about Alex's draft notice: in all those years of war, he was the first boy in our town to get drafted. Soon men were coming into the store and seizing Alex's hand in both of theirs, their eyes rich with pride, and all those girls who had a crush on him but whom he never asked out loved him even more, and they would love him most if he came back dead.

That was the summer he wore chaps while working in the store. Fringed batwing chaps, an open-crown black hat, and nubby ostrich boots. Spurs on the boots, sometimes. My father had ordered the chaps a long time before, perhaps romantically fantasizing the day when some weary wrangler might hitch his horse to the bumper out front and lay his eyes on them through the window. But my mother said the chaps were hiding the Fritos, and she had him put them back in storage. We sell chips here, not chaps, she said.

Alex wiped the greasy dust off the leather and fastened them to his thighs.

"Now, why?" my mother said when she saw him in his getup.

"Give the tourists a thrill?" he suggested.

It was the middle of June, and the Tombstone Race was coming up. In the Tombstone Race, folks raced with eighty-pound replicas of Billy the Kid's gravestone on their backs, and we got a few extra gawkers in town for that. Alex had planned to run the race again that year. No one so far had found it in them to mention the ghoulishness of his running around with a tombstone on his back just before he was to go off to war.

My father kept an eye on Alex in his chaps. Ever since I could remember, he'd had this watchfulness toward him. He never criticized, just watched. It was anybody's guess what he thought, about Alex or about most anything else. This poker face was what had made him a good player in his day—though in the end bad luck caught up with him, and after marrying my mother he'd given up gambling.

Alex's problem, in my mother's opinion, was that he was slow in developing to maturity. He needed something to make him outgrow what she called his "silliness." His going to war would surely do the job.

My father wasn't okay with Alex's being drafted. Not that he said anything about it, but I knew it troubled him. When those men came in to congratulate Alex, saying, "Do us proud, son," my father looked away and wiped a counter or fronted the bread.

Elmo was not one of the men who told Alex to "do us proud." Elmo was against the war, which might seem strange for the owner of a macho-man bar, but then Elmo was what people called a "freethinker."

A few days after Alex got his draft notice, Elmo came into our store and invited him to the bar for a drink.

"You know he's not old enough to go to bars," my father said.

"If he's old enough to go to war, I guess he's old enough to have a beer," Elmo replied.

Alex twirled on his stool and grinned. Alex didn't get out much. He'd had a regular number of friends in high school, but they had all paired off with girls and gotten married, and now they hung together as couples, some of them already with babies.

That night he came home smelling of beer. My mother, who hadn't been at the store when Elmo extended his invitation, remarked on it.

My father used Elmo's exact words: "If he's old enough to go to war, I guess he's old enough to have a beer."

You had to wonder why Elmo would risk his new liquor license by serving someone underage. Twenty-one was the minimum drinking age in New Mexico. But I guess Elmo knew that the community was willing to allow Billy's (which, after all, was named for a famous outlaw) an occasional dispensation from the rules, especially in a case like this. So for that night, Alex was an honorary twenty-one. Twenty-one, I might add, also had a certain mystique with regard to Billy the Kid. Billy the Kid was famously gunned down at age twenty-one, and supposedly he'd killed twenty-one men, one for every year of his life.

Billy's Bar was good for the whole town, economically speaking. People came to it from as far away as Albuquerque and Amarillo and who knows where else, on their motorcycles. Many of the invariably muscular men sported big handlebar moustaches and wore lots of leather, while the women, who had motorcycles of their own, favored denim and plaid. Most of the motorcycles were elegant machines, Harleys and Triumphs and Nortons and a few vintage Indians. We locals pretty much let them have the place, and nobody disparaged them. The worst people called them was "tough customers," which was actually more praise than anything, because the operative word here was "customers." Those folks not only spent money at Billy's, they bought gas, and meat for their barbeques, and they visited the Kid's grave and went to the museum, and sometimes they stayed at local motels, though mostly they camped. They rarely got rowdy, or not so rowdy that anybody'd have to call the law, anyway.

On the afternoon following Alex's visit to Billy's, one such customer pulled up to our gas island on a thundering Harley chopper. Nailed in place by the ungodly hammering of the big v-twin engine, I stood and watched him. The man braced his feet on the ground, took off his helmet, and shook his long, Indian-black hair around his shoulders. Then he shut off the thunder, dismounted, and filled his tank with regular.

He was a young, lanky man, someone my parents would have called a "hippie" a couple of years earlier, but by now, early seventies, even my parents knew that there were as many redneck longhairs as hippie ones. The whole hair issue was so confusing that they simply withheld judgment on men with long hair.

The young biker carried his helmet by his side. It was painted the same as the motorcycle's gas tank, purple candy-cane swirls over white. I remember Alex once telling me that real outlaw bikers, like Hell's Angels, refused to wear those "brain buckets."

When he entered, he said "Hey" to Alex, who was sitting on his usual stool behind the register, and they shook hands. They knew each other, I guessed from Billy's Bar.

Despite his hangover, Alex had been practicing that morning for the Tombstone Race by running around the backyard with a rough slab of shale on his back, and for the last couple of hours he'd been acting too sore to get off his stool. But now he perked right up and followed the biker down the canned-goods aisle.

He asked the guy if he could help him, the guy made a reply I couldn't hear, and they laughed. Alex had one hand shoved in the back pocket of his Wranglers and he pushed his butt out a little when he laughed.

The guy put a can of crabmeat and a box of Triscuits in his helmet and said that would do it. Alex brushed past me and got behind the register to check the guy out.

Crabmeat was one of those items, like the chaps and the *Uniforms of the World* book, that my father occasionally ordered on a whim but that never sold. This impulse was what remained of his old gambling days, I guess. Prior to marrying my mother, he'd lost everything in private poker games. Now it seemed like bad luck was still following him, what with his son getting a losing number in the draft lottery. The lottery reminded me of a story we'd read that year in high school called, in fact, "The Lottery," in which every year a whole town chose lots to see which family would get stoned to death.

Alex wiped the dust off the can of crabmeat with a tissue and rang it up.

"Go for a spin?" the guy said.

At that moment my parents came out of the office, where they had been doing the quarterly taxes. Alex swallowed and glanced at my father. My father gazed out at the bike listing in the cool shadow of the overhang.

"Not without a helmet," he said.

The biker placed the helmet on Alex's head.

"Fit?" he said.

"Yeah," Alex said shyly.

My mother had watched Alex run around the yard that morning with the stone on his back, her face a stone itself. As far as she was concerned, he had to go to war, and that was all there was to it. She came from a line of warriors. Both her grandfathers had fought on the side of the Regulators in the turf war known as the Lincoln County War, the same outfit Billy the Kid fought for. In other words, she came from people who would have understood Nixon's arguments for "peace with honor" in Vietnam, because things hadn't gone well for the Regulators either, and in the end that conflict, too, boiled down to issues of pride and saving face.

Her Regulator grandparents managed to negotiate a settlement with the enemy and held on to some of their land and cattle, but years later the family received another blow to its pride when my mother and her brothers found themselves obliged, for financial reasons, to sell the last of the ranch to the big feedlot operators. Soon afterward she and my father opened the Circle K franchise using the money from that sale. The fact that a K inside a circle—her maiden name was Kyle—had been the brand of her ranch was an irony not lost on her. I figured the only reason she let Alex prance around the store in chaps, which might seem to make a further mockery of our ranching past, was that soon enough he'd be off to Vietnam, so there was no point in making an issue of it now.

That he'd soon be drafted was also the reason she didn't object to his going off to ride around with this biker, I suspected. Plus the fact that she, like everyone else in our neck of the woods, believed that "boys will be boys," and that a little badness in young men was a good thing. This was Billy the Kid country, after all.

So she stood by stoically—it was funny the way she could put on the same poker face as my dad—and watched as Alex fastened the straps of the motorcycle helmet to his chin and then bent over to untie his chaps.

"Leave those things on," the biker said. "Sweetheart's got a hot tail pipe."

The biker, whose name was Corey, had a great smile: big, white, even teeth, like Peter Fonda's in *Easy Rider*, whom he kind of resembled, long jaw and all. Alex rode with Corey the rest of the day. And he rode with him the next day, and the next. As I filled the slush machine and loaded corn dogs and did other chores normally assigned to Alex, I thought about them plunging and soaring along the dippy road to Nara Visa, making the pheasants and prairie chickens burst from the buffalo grass, or blasting into the red-earth cotton country of Texas or toward the blue mountains of Santa Fe, fleeing the anvil clouds that rose with such astonishing verticality that time of year, and I softly sang "Born to Be Wild" until my father said, "All right, Bunny."

Alex didn't talk much about his adventures, but the light in his eyes told of private marvels. He was full of restlessness now, a nervous energy that my mother didn't like.

On the morning of the fourth day of his adventuring he announced, in the kitchen of our home, plans to go camping with Corey for a couple of nights in the Sangre de Cristo mountains. He told us this as he minced onion and pepper for our Denver omelet. Whenever we wanted an omelet, Alex made it. He was our omelet man.

"Just don't forget where you have to be on the seventeenth," my mother said brusquely.

The seventeenth, we all knew, was the day he had to present himself for his armed forces physical. My father planned to drive him to Albuquerque for it.

Alex was already in his chaps and waiting for Corey to come by the house to pick him up. He scraped the ingredients into the skillet and gently folded the egg over them. When the omelet was done he slid it onto the big blue Fiestaware platter he always served his omelets on and placed the platter before us on the table. He stared out the kitchen window, fists on the counter, and said, "I'm not going."

"Oh, sure, you can go, son," said my father, giving my mother a don't-be-a-spoilsport look.

"No. I mean I'm not going to be inducted."

I had grabbed the spatula to cut a piece of the omelet, and now I put it down. Everyone waited for Alex to explain what he meant. Had the Selective Service made some mistake regarding his draft lottery number? Had he discovered he had flat feet? Was the war over?

"I'm refusing," he said.

"Refusing what, son?" said my father.

69

"The draft."

"Why, Alex, that's desertion," my mother said in a danger-ously even-toned voice.

Outside the window, in a distant field, stood an idle harrow, its clawed arms lifted as if in supplication to the sky.

"Now hold on," my father said. "Nobody's talking about desertion."

"Well," said Alex, "there's conscientious objection, but you go to prison for that, and I don't want to go to prison. There's deferments for students and parents and preachers, but I'm not any of those. So what's left is what I'm doing."

This didn't sound like the Alex we knew, the Alex whose "silliness" would be cured, in my mother's opinion, by his going to war. This was a decisive, serious Alex—an Alex already "cured," as it were. We all stared at him.

Corey came up the street then on his booming motorcycle, made all the louder because he'd taken off the baffles to give it more horsepower. A sound that jumped the heart. Alex slung his pack over his back and went out the door and swung his leg over the motorcycle seat and looped his arms around Corey's middle and they took off.

I reached again for the spatula but my mother stopped my hand. She got up, took the platter, and dumped the omelet into the garbage.

Elmo came into the store that afternoon. By then my mother had had time to think about Alex's announcement. ("A draft dodger," she said, while my father held his silence. "In my fam-ily. Well, well, well.") Certainly Corey was the main culprit—and I knew she regretted now not having confronted him that morning when he thundered up to our front door. But Elmo was responsible for inviting Alex to Billy's, where he had pre-sumably met this motorcycle boy. So Elmo had some account-ing to do.

I was at the gas pumps refilling the squeegee water and didn't hear the initial exchange between my mother and Elmo, but when I came into the store my father said to them, "Let's go in the back to discuss this. Bunny, take care of the register."

My parents' words were indistinguishable, but some of Elmo's exclamations reached me. "*Zero* tolerance," he boomed at one point. "Zero!" I punched in an extra zero and the customer I was checking out, who seemed oblivious to the argument in the back, said, "Twenty dollars is mighty steep for Vy-eena sausages, honey."

The customer left. A lull, and then a commotion, something tumbling from the office desk, a smacking sound, and my father's voice, "There *there*." Elmo stormed out of the office and out of the store, his face on fire. He mashed the starter of his Harley and roared off. My mother emerged from the office pale as ice, my father behind her, gray lipped.

That night, with no customers and their Vienna sausages to distract me, I listened closely to my parents' bedroom discussion, my head right at their door.

"I'd rather he be dead," she said, "than be one of *those*."

"I can't believe you think that. I don't believe you think that, Jolene."

Silence followed, a minute or two of it. Then he said, "If he goes off to the war he might well come back dead. Would you like that? How could a mother ever send a son to war? Any son."

"Oh, my Lord. No wonder he's the way he is. Maybe it'd teach him something about being a man, since you haven't."

I suppose some men in my father's place might have hit her then, to show her that he wasn't going to tolerate her impugning his own manliness by suggesting he'd failed to teach his son to be a man. But then, a real man doesn't hit a woman, does he?

"You heard what Elmo said," said my father. "Zero tolerance. He'd be despised for . . . for what he is. That's what they'd teach him in the service, to hate himself."

"Goddamn Elmo. Goddamn *you*. If you hadn't let Alex go to that fucking bar" (I'd never heard my mother swear like this before) "he never would've met this, this *Corey*. Did *you* know what kind of a place it was when you let him go? You did, didn't you?"

"No," said my father. "No, Jolene, I didn't."

This amazed me. Everybody knew it was a motorcycle bar. What were they talking about? It occurs to me now that my parents were perhaps the first locals to realize that Billy's wasn't just a motorcycle bar, that it was something else besides. That it was a gathering place for *those* people—though it wasn't at all clear to me then who *those* people were or what Alex was. In the course of their conversation with Elmo, in asking him about Corey and Alex, in hearing his passionate argument against the military and how it treated *those* people (how would Elmo have referred to them?) they must have realized it.

For Elmo to have invited her vulnerable and immature son into his den of iniquity, perhaps actually introduced him to this Corey—this was, to her, unforgivable. Now Alex was out running around with, spending the night with, with this . . . well. Who on top of everything else was advising him to dodge the draft.

"You're the father," she said finally. "You talk to him for once. Because I'm telling you, I'm not going to have my family dishonored by this."

That Sunday was the day of the Tombstone Race. By morning, Alex still hadn't returned from his camping trip. We went about our work at the Circle K in heavy silence. It was one of the busiest days of the year at the store, with plenty of customers to distract us. None of us mentioned Alex, either to speculate as to whether he'd be back to run the race or to complain that he wasn't at the store to give a hand, but all our movements grew stiff with unease.

By noon we were running low on change and small denominations.

"Here's some big ones," my father said, sticking a roll of bills into my pocket. "See what you can scare up."

The banks were closed that day, it being a Sunday and all, so I'd have to bug other merchants for change. This was bad form in my mother's eyes, because it showed poor planning on our part, though on the other hand it proved business was good at our store, with lots of customers brandishing big bills. I fingered the roll as I walked toward town. The June sun blazed directly overhead, and I cast no shadow. The cicadas, having sputtered through the coolness of the morning, hit their high and steady heat-of-the-day pitch.

The roll felt awfully fat in my pocket. I pulled it out and counted it. Five hundred dollars! All in fifties and twenties. Surely we didn't need *that* much change? I might have turned back and asked my father about it had I not heard cheering from the football field. The Tombstone Race was underway. I had to see it, and see if Alex had made it.

A word about the Tombstone Race. The race was a peculiar idea born of the controversies surrounding Billy the Kid's gravesite and of the multiple thefts of his headstone. The truth is, no one really knew where the Kid was buried since the Pecos River flood of 1904 had washed lots of bodies out of their graves and mixed everything up in the cemetery. That could be anyone reburied under the Kid's stone, maybe even one of our own relatives.

Then there was the problem of the headstone itself. It was stolen in 1950, but in any case that wasn't the original wooden marker, which had been lost in the flood. What marked his grave now, which like I say might have been anybody's grave, was a replica of the replacement headstone. The "real" headstone wasn't recovered until 1976, in Granbury, Texas, a town famous for sheltering aging outlaws who had faked their deaths, including Brushy Bill Roberts, who claimed to be Billy the Kid himself. (But then so did an ancient rancher from Ramah, New Mexico, named John Miller.) To further complicate things, the Billy the Kid Museum downtown had a gravesite for the Kid identical to the one behind the *other* museum, whose sign proclaimed it to be the "Authentic 'Real'

Gravesite of Billy the Kid." At both sites, the Kid's headstone read, "The Boy Bandit King. He Died As He Had Lived." His grave(s) was (were) flanked by those of two other men, whose stones read, simply, "Pals."

Speaking of pals: as I got to the football field, I heard the boom-blat of a Harley and turned to see Corey and Alex ride into the parking lot. They dismounted and stretched lengthily, laughing with the effort. Alex took off his chaps and touched his toes and did some jumping jacks. He was warming up for the race.

The women's race had already taken place. Their stones weighed only forty pounds. Edith Wurlitzer had won again, but that was predictable. She was thirty years old but her heart was 20 percent larger than normal, so she was a freak of nature. No way I was ever going to race as long as Edith Wurlitzer was in the running.

The big event was the open-to-all eighty-pound-stone race. That's the one Alex was in. He ambled down with a saddlesore gait to the judge's booth and signed the waiver absolving the town and school of any responsibility for crushed vertebrae and smashed toes. The bleachers were packed: lots of families with children, waves and shouts and laughter. Scattered among the spectators were groups of motorcycle people, most of them, because of the heat, shed of their leather and denim, the men's massive muscles rippling under their T-shirts, and they too seemed happy, saluting each other across the field, soda cans gripped in their big paws—beer was prohibited at this event, a restriction they seem to have cheerfully accepted. In the parking lot, their row of "machines," as they liked to call them, slanted in the same direction, glistening.

Alex clowned around on the track, to the whistles and cheers of the spectators. He removed his western shirt strip-tease style, unsnapping each button with a flourish before tossing it to the side. He kept his ribbed undershirt on, but there was no way he was going to be able to run in his boots, so he took them off too, and his socks—but after he felt how hot the macadam was, he put the socks back on. That's what he was going to run his race in: undershirt, jeans, and socks.

None of the other competitors seemed to be taking the race very seriously either. One of them was dressed as a rodeo clown. A couple of them, predictably enough, were got up as the Kid, baggy pants, revolvers (hopefully toy), and all, and they both kept their boots on. The only runner who seemed truly serious was our high school's star running back, who was dressed in full football regalia, including his helmet. Edith of the giant heart decided to contend, the only woman in this race, but she was a small woman and had to have two men place the slab carefully over her scrawny shoulders, not a good sign.

The starter fired his pistol and off they went. There were two hurdles you had to throw the stone over, and then you had to pick it up and keep running. You and your tombstone had to stay within your narrow lane or you were disqualified, and this was the running back's downfall, for in his show-offy might he tossed his stone too far, into the clown's lane. The clown paused to squat profanely over the unamused jock's rock, much to the hilarity of the children in the stands. The Billy the Kids tottered in their boots, going nowhere. Edith staggered like a drunk and keeled over before reaching the first hurdle. A couple of burly oil-field types handled their rocks with ease, but they weren't used to running and were soon winded.

And then there was Alex, my brother Alex, energized by his recent adventures, by his new friendship, by the prospect, it seemed, of a whole new life. That boy tossed his tombstone, picked it up (using the strength of his legs, as our father trained us to do with heavy boxes at the store), galloped down the track, tossed again, picked up, galloped—and won.

At the finish line he raised the tombstone over his head, all eighty pounds of it, and with a roar he hurled it onto the football field, where it broke in two, like Moses's tablet of commandments. The crowd roared back.

Some of the same men who had congratulated him when he'd gotten his draft notice now strode up and congratulated him on his victory. Soon the motorcycle folk gathered around him. They slapped him on the ass like football players do to scoring teammates. They put their heads together for low-voiced jokes, rearing back with laughter at the punch lines. Corey slapped Alex on the ass too, but his hand remained there just a moment too long, and that's when things finally started to come together in my slow, naïve, small-town, sixteen-year-old brain. *Those* people.

I felt weak in the knees, and I sat back down on the bleachers. I guess I always knew that my brother was . . . no, I didn't know what I knew. All I knew was that I couldn't turn away from him. What I had to do, what I must do, was find out if he still intended to dodge the draft—and if he did, I had to give him that five hundred dollars I had in my pocket. I wondered if this had been my father's idea all along, that I should find him and give him this money and send him on his way.

I approached the group and told Alex I needed to talk to him. The others grew silent. Corey tossed him the keys to his bike and told us to go for a spin. Alex was still in his socks; they were the filthiest socks I'd ever seen.

I kicked off my sandals and stripped my feet of their socks, pink ones with white bunnies. "Here," I said, "wear mine. You always said socks and sandals were the tackiest combination on earth anyway."

Alex put on my socks and his boots. Corey took Alex's dirty socks.

"We'll auction them," Corey said. "The champ's socks."

Alex and I walked out of the bowl of the football field.

"That takes a lot of trust, a guy letting you drive his bike," said Alex.

"Great," I said, a little sarcastically.

Two helmets hung on the motorcycle, the familiar purple-striped one and one Alex had bought for himself, solid teal, a color he'd always liked. It looked like half of a giant bird's egg.

"I don't need a brain bucket," I said. "I'll just let my freak flag fly."

Alex laughed. "Put it on, dear sister. We're not the Hell's Angels. And watch that tail pipe."

I put on his teal helmet and he put on Corey's and we boomed past First Baptist and headed east on the highway. I didn't ask where we were going. His belly was firm and it felt nice hugging him. My brother was always sexy as hell, even if he was my brother.

We took the turnoff to the "Authentic 'Real' Gravesite of Billy the Kid," which was also the road Billy's Bar was on. Already three or four motorcycles were parked in its dusty lot, under the elms. We continued south, the deep-green alfalfa fields spreading out on either side of us, watered by the Pecos River. At the cemetery Alex shut down the engine and we got off the bike. The only sound now was the monotonous song of the cicadas.

It was a forlorn, sunbaked cemetery, containing only the presumed remains of Billy the Kid, his two pals, the grave of one "Lucian Maxwell, Frontiersman," and one or two others decorated with small, faded-orange plastic flowers. A couple of fat raindrops fell from a single black cloud and struck the dust like bullets, and then the cloud drifted away.

"You know who made this cemetery, don't you?" Alex asked.

"Not really."

"The US Army. And you know who for, don't you?"

"Soldiers?"

"Twenty-one of them."

"Where are they now?"

"They took them to the National Cemetery in Santa Fe."

I supposed I remembered this vaguely from school.

"And you know what the army was doing here in the first place, don't you?"

"The fort?"

"And what was the fort for?"

"Well, it was a fort! To protect against the Indians and stuff."

"Yeah, protect. You know who they kept over there?" He pointed to a pasture where two spotted horses grazed.

"Who?"

"Ten thousand, five hundred Indians. Ten thousand Navajos and five hundred Apaches. All taken from their homes, forced to march across the badlands, and penned up right there like cattle. That was what the fort was for. To imprison them. You know how many of them died?"

"A lot?"

"Three thousand. Three thousand and finally they said fuck 'em and sent the survivors home. Then they closed down the fort and end of story. I bet they haven't taught you that at school."

"Not yet."

"Not yet. Not ever I bet. And you don't think they took those three thousand Indians and buried them in Santa Fe, do you? It's just like fuckin' Vietnam. Go over there, kill a bunch of gooks, then say fuck it, we're outta here.

"I'm not going into the military, you know. I sure as shit am not. Corey was in the Army. He told me all about it."

"What are you going to do?"

"We're going to Canada."

My stomach dropped. Canada! That was a straight shot up the prairie, but a very long straight shot.

And then I remembered the five hundred dollars. I handed him the roll.

"I'm not going to take this from you, Bunny."

"It's not mine."

"Where'd you get it?"

"It's from the store."

"Well, take it back. I'll be fine. I've got friends."

"No, keep it. Dad wants you to have it. Really."

"Oh yeah?" He looked out to the alfalfa fields. "But he doesn't have the, the what it takes, to give it to me himself."

"I don't *know*," I said. "Just *take* it."

He flicked the edges of the roll as he gazed out at the field. Then he slipped it into his boot, beneath my sock.

We stood and looked at each other for a moment, and I felt my eyes get hot and my throat swell. We fell into each other's arms. I caught a whiff of his French moustache wax—that strange, foreign fragrance.

"When are you coming back?" I mumbled into his shoulder.

"When all this blows over," he said.

I didn't know what he thought was going to blow over, or if he was just saying this to comfort me. The war would end, of course, but the wounds would remain. It was hard to imagine that our mother, for one, would ever get over either his desertion of that war or his becoming one of *those* people.

Alex let me off a block from our Circle K and boomed back to the football field to catch up with his people. I slipped into the store through the back door. It was still busy, but my parents no longer seemed to be hurting for change; somehow that problem had been solved, perhaps simply by asking people to pay with small bills. I busied myself refilling the sugar dispensers and tidying up the coffee nook.

It's strange how a store can be chockablock busy one minute and suddenly devoid of customers the next. It was in one of those lulls that my mother at last noticed my presence.

"Well, finally! Did you bring that change?"

My father's face gave nothing away. It was impossible for me to tell whether he was complicit in what I had done with the money. If so, he wasn't going to admit it yet. At that moment I realized how afraid he was of my mother.

"I gave it to him," I said. "I saw Alex, and I gave it to him."

"You what, now?" she said.

My father stepped in then. "He earned it, Jolene."

"Not yet he hadn't," she said. Technically she was right: he and I both had gotten paid the day before he started riding around with Corey.

"Well, you can dock my pay until it's paid," I said.

My mother didn't seem to hear this. She stared at the phone, her face as hard as I've ever seen it, and I wondered if she was truly capable of doing what it flashed through my mind she might do: call the sheriff, report the money embezzled, and have Alex held until the army got hold of him. Because as far as she was concerned, it was better to have an outlaw son, even one that stole from his own family's business, than a cowardly deserter of a son, one who ran off "riding bitch" on another man's motorcycle. I hated to think this, but I did, and I believed her only hesitation was knowing that if she did report it, it would come out that he'd taken the money precisely to fund this desertion, and that I, and possibly my father as well, had been complicit in it.

"Well, I don't think we're gonna get it back from him now," I said. "He's run off with the Hell's Angels, and even the law doesn't want to mess with that bunch."

I amazed myself with these words. Where had this sudden idea come from? My parents stared at me with astonishment. When I realized what a stroke of genius it was, I began to babble an elaboration.

"I thought that guy Corey was on his own, just a lone biker. I guess we all did, right? But then I see him and Alex with all those Angels. I mean, I was kind of scared, you know? Those guys are *out*laws. I mean, they're *famous* outlaws. Of course, me being the sister and all, they treated me real good. Alex, they really like him. And like, they really take care of their own, you know?"

Whether she believed me or not—and I was pretty sure my father didn't, though he kept that poker face—it made a good story, a story she could use. Because to have a son who joined the *Hell's Angels*—that put things on a whole new level. She didn't have a sissy son now—she had a true outlaw son.

The question was, would the town believe it? That's where Elmo stepped in to help, bless his heart. I always suspected that my father put him up to it, but I guess I'll never know, now that my father's passed away and Elmo's who knows where. In any case, Elmo told anyone who asked, "Yep, Alex Beaumont rode out with the Hell's Angels, and as far as anyone knows, he's riding with them still."

Meanwhile, my mother did her part. Anybody'd ask about Alex, and she'd tell them the same thing. Those men who had congratulated Alex on his getting drafted shook their heads as if to say what a shame, but you could tell they were impressed. The Hell's Angels! That's probably the outfit Billy the Kid would belong to if he were alive today.

She kept to the story when a couple of men from the Selective Service in skinny ties showed up to inquire about Alex. Gone off with the Angels, she told them. The men gazed at their black shoes for what they considered a decent interval, then asked if they could see the death certificate, "for their records."

"Gone off with the Hell's Angels, is what I mean," she said, her head cocked defiantly. My father closed his eyes.

The truth was, the Hell's Angels had never been in our town, as far as anybody actually knew. Nor had any other outlaw biker gang, for that matter. But if Elmo said so, and said Alex rode off with them, it must be true. He should know: it was he who ran the biker bar, after all.

As it happened, the rumor became the downfall of Billy's. Because before long, the Bandidos showed up at the place. The Bandidos were a Southwest motorcycle gang and archenemies of the Angels. They'd heard the rumor, and they showed up en masse. They wanted any and all Angels off their New Mexico turf. They rode in on their ape-hanger choppers, the sleeves torn from the sockets of their denim jackets, twenty or thirty gap-toothed, greasy, long-haired horrors ready to rumble. I don't know what they made of the buffed bikes in Billy's lot, but the fact that they didn't see a single Angel or any other biker flying gang colors confused them, which gave most customers a chance to discreetly leave. Those that didn't get out fast enough they chased out with swings of their motorcycle chains. And then they made the place theirs.

They drank up Elmo's beer without paying, puked on the floor, and carved "Bandidos" hugely on the bar. Elmo evidently made no effort to convince them that the Angels had in fact never been there, much less explain to them the whole complicated story of how the rumor came to be, how it was concocted to preserve the dignity of a family whose son's manliness was in question. Maybe he thought they were too addled to listen to all that, but more likely, knowing Elmo, he was simply too brave to blow our family's cover.

They stayed the whole afternoon and didn't leave until midnight. Maybe Elmo thought he'd seen the last of them, but he was wrong. They returned the following Saturday and hung out just as long, though this time they tried to act more civil. They actually paid this time, and the leader made a kind of apology for the previous week's abuse, though no doubt it was one of those tough-guy apologies that makes you feel he's doing you a favor by offering it. It seems they had decided to make Billy's their place, a permanent Bandido hangout or hideout.

The regular customers, those mustachioed leather people with the glittering motorcycles, disappeared completely. Elmo at that point must have decided that his bar was never going to be the same and that he might as well do something drastic, which was to greet the Bandidos, the next time they came, with the business end of a shotgun.

The Bandidos scrambled off the property pronto, then spent an hour or two roaring up and down the road in front of Billy's in a face-saving parade of bravado.

"I hope Elmo's insurance on that place is up to date," more than one customer said to my parents at the store. My father looked plainly pained at that, my mother triumphant.

I know it hurt my father forever afterward that he didn't offer Elmo some kind of help to protect Billy's against the barbarians, who, after all, would never have shown up in the first place if Elmo hadn't confirmed the rumor, sparked by me, that the Angels had been hanging out there. Certainly no townsfolk, even the sheriff, cared to get involved. This was Elmo's problem. Nobody had asked him to bring a tough-guy bar to town, and now that it had come to this, well, he had made his bed and he had to lie in it.

Elmo lived in town, three miles from his bar, and it was unlikely that he heard the Bandido motorcycles from his literal bed the night of the fire. It's possible they even came in trucks, for the sake of stealth as well as for carrying the gasoline with which they burned Billy's down. The arson investigators concluded only that a good deal of "accelerant" had been used, and certainly the place burned thoroughly, pieces of stucco shooting all the way to the highway, and the booze bottles the Bandidos hadn't managed to carry off exploded too, giving the ash a kind of licorice scent. The Billy the Kid cutout etched a silhouette of itself on the floor when it burned. The only area that didn't burn thoroughly was the basement, where the investigators found several sets of smoke-blackened handcuffs and some inexplicable sling-like leather contraptions, as well as various mysterious rings screwed into the walls. The investigators, city men from Albuquerque and who knows where else, made no comment on what these objects might have been used for, but it was clear to our community that bikers, Hell's Angels or Bandidos or whoever, were using the place to imprison and even torture their enemies. Billy's Bar was a much more sinister place than anyone had suspected.

Elmo, big laugh and bright eyes notwithstanding, was definitely persona non grata in our town then. He didn't stay much longer. People said he went to join the San Francisco Hell's Angels, but nobody really knew.

"Good riddance to that savage," is all my mother had to say.

As for Alex, he and Corey settled in Vancouver. It wasn't much of a place for motorcycle riding, what with all the rain—they had up there what our Pueblo Indians call "female" rain, gentle and steady, as opposed to the more typical "male" thunderstorms of New Mexico—but they seemed happy. They opened a little French-style café that became locally famous for Alex's omelets. My father and I—though never my mother—went to visit them several times. They had heard what had happened to Billy's, but to this day I don't know if they knew their role in it, that is, if they knew the problem began when I started the rumor that they were members of the Hell's Angels, all so that my mother could have the satisfaction of telling people she had an outlaw son rather than a sissy one.

Over the years Alex grew immensely muscular—every time I hugged him, it was like hugging an ever-larger sculpture of hard flesh. He grew a moustache, one of those giant Fu Manchus popular in those Village People days, for which he no longer needed wax. So I stopped getting a whiff of that exotic moustache wax when I embraced him. But if I wanted to remind myself of him in the old days, all I had to do was take out the tiny-toothed moustache combs he'd left behind—they were still in the medicine cabinet: the fake-ivory one, the wooden one, the plastic one with the brush opposite the teeth, such delicate implements for such a symbol of virility—and sniff them, and it would all come back to me, that summer when Alex became a man.

Their Songs

RUSTY FINISHES THE set with a new song he's written, "Their Song." The song's about a man who's having an affair with another woman. One afternoon, lying in the motel bed with this other woman, the man begins to cry. The woman, with great concern, asks him why he's crying, and he confesses that it's because the song playing on the motel radio is his and his wife's favorite—"their" song. In fact, it's not; he's never heard it before, and he and his wife don't even have a song. But it's a nice song, it moves him, and he likes this new woman a lot, and he thinks she'll like him better if he shows some sensitivity about what he's doing to his wife by having an affair. Maybe this new woman will run off with him if she sees he's the kind of man who takes these things to heart, that he doesn't take them lightly.

The man hasn't really thought it through, though, and his lover tells him (a) that the song's too new to be his and his wife's song, (b) that he'd better think before he bullshines, (c) that it's a lousy song anyway, and (d) that if he misses his wife so much, he can just go back to her. And with that, the new woman leaves the motel. The man goes home. And there he finds his wife listening to that same song, and she likes it as much as he does, and he realizes who he really loves, and it becomes their song and they live happily ever after.

When the set's over, Rusty looks around the honky-tonk carefully for his wife Tammy. Tammy's not there, of course, so he goes and sits with Geraldine, who's at a wobbly table near the stage. The waitress brings him a longneck.

Geraldine's been sipping margaritas. She holds his hand and tells him it's a beautiful song. Then she asks him how he got the idea for it.

"Well," says Rusty, "that actually happened."

"To who?"

"Friend of mine. Except the last part. The happily ever after."

Geraldine licks salt from the edge of her glass.

"So who's this friend?"

"Just this guy I know."

She lets go of his hand. "You know a lot of bullshiners?"

"Who doesn't? But anyway, his tears were real. Just his timing was off."

"Were they? Real tears?"

"Sure. He really thought he loved this new woman, and he figured if he cried he'd get to keep her. Women love a sensitive man. But he loved his wife too."

"So why didn't they live happily ever after?"

"That's another story. Another song."

She takes a long sip of her drink and says, "Hey, Rusty? How come I've never seen you cry?"

"Maybe I'm not a bullshiner."

"Maybe you don't love me."

"Aw, honey."

"Maybe you don't want to keep me."

He reaches for her hand, but she pulls it away. He looks into her eyes, tears moistening his own. She downs the rest of her drink and jumps up, rocking the table.

"Sure, Rusty. You know something? Your timing's way off. Maybe you better go back to Tammy. If she'll have you."

He starts after her, but she pushes him away. He feels the audience watching him. He sits back down. He drinks his beer. He watches some guy go up to Geraldine at the bar and start bullshining her. He wonders where Tammy might be. He imagines a man and his wife each having an affair and each hearing "Their Song" on the radio when they're with their respective lovers and crying when they hear it. Their lovers leave them, just like in the song. The man and wife go to a bar to drink away their sorrows, and they encounter one another there as if for the first time. The band is playing, of course, "Their Song." Timing's everything. And speaking of which, the break's over, and the audience is impatient for the next set.

The Extra

MY NAME IS Dwayne Brock, and I'm the last convict here at Old Main. Okay, I'm not exactly a con, because this prison has been de-commed, or shall I say de-conned, and is now leased to the film industry as a set. All the other prisoners have been moved to the North Unit, a super-modern, high-surveillance facility where you can't touch your visitors and you have to read your mail from a TV monitor.

Warden Johnson sometimes introduces me to the movie people as the caretaker of the old joint, though once I heard him refer to me as a "guest" of the penal system, or maybe it was "ghost." Like any cop, the warden can be an ironical asshole, but at least he's been flexible enough to go along with movie director Roger Rudman's idea to let me live here and work on projects, which is what movie folks call movies. I help build sets—like any second-story man, I can handle a tool—and sometimes I serve as a consultant on questions about prison life. What I like best is acting, as Roger and the warden both know. I've been given roles as an extra, or what Roger calls atmosphere acting, in the last two pictures filmed here, *Lockdown* and *Bloodsport*.

This is the story of how I came to get this gig.

I was released from this very prison, the Penitentiary of New Mexico's Old Main, just before it was decommissioned and leased. It was the day after my sixty-first birthday. "Have you made any arrangements, Dwayne?" the warden asked me as I signed the release forms. Warden Johnson is one of those buddy-buddy white shirts who calls prisoners by their first names. The New Mexico Department of Corrections hired him after the riot to improve inmate-administration relations. I've even heard him call a prisoner a "resident," and I don't think he meant it ironically.

"Arrangements?" I said. At the moment, the only arrangement I could feature was me between a lady's—any lady's—legs.

"Some kind of work? Place to stay?"

"None of your goddamned business," I said, signing with a flourish. I was styling big, trying to hide my own nervousness about getting out.

He didn't push it. He knew I'd topped out my sentence and didn't owe him an accounting of my plans for the future. I'd done my time. Done every minute of every hour of every day. No parole or halfway house for me. I was flat-out free.

Cons who top out their sentences usually do so because they've lost all their good time due to bad behavior or because they make such a lousy case for themselves before the parole board it's afraid to let them out. The reason I went the limit was my NKRC classification. NKRC means No Known Relatives or Concerned. No one to release me to, no one to meet me at the gate.

Some of my fellow prisoners, when they learned I was going to top out, believed I had fallen through the cracks. They even began to call me Roach on that account. They thought the administration had forgotten about me, and they promised to bring it to the white shirts' attention. But that kind of falling between the cracks only happens in busy county jails, not in the Big House. Here they have plenty of time to know who you are and where you're at.

The chief psychologist knew all about me, or thought he did. He'd diagnosed my personality as "refractory," which the dictionary defines as "obstinately resistant to authority or control." He made his diagnosis on the basis of a psychological test in which I was supposed to say as many different words beginning with *A* as I could in one minute. I'd heard about this little test, which you flunked if you couldn't think of a lot of different words. I asked him if I could try it with *F*. He said go ahead, even though he knew I was fucking with him. So I went at it: fuck you, fucker, fuck face, fucking fuck. . . . I was fucking with him. But then, he was fucking with me. We were fucking with each other, but it was all to a purpose: I was NKRC, and we were both afraid of me getting out. So we were making sure the evaluation went badly. He looked at me with a little smile and said, "Anything else? Foresight, maybe?"

"Fuck, forgot foresight," I said.

"Well, that's a problem," he said, hanging on to that smile. "No foresight. Can't foresee the consequences of your actions."

But he was wrong about that, and he knew it. I could well see the consequences of fucking with him. I was going to top out my sentence. "Felon forfeits freedom," I said as I walked back to my cell.

Film. Now there's a fine four-letter word. I'm very pleased to be in film, even though there are some aspects of it that I don't get. For example, I don't see why we're building phony cellblocks out of plywood. Why do we need fake cells when we have these real ones all around? That aside, I have to say the industry impresses me. All those scenes shot out of order and then smoothed together into a single motion picture. I admire it. It takes foresight.

Anyway: I'm in the warden's office, signing my release papers, when the warden steps outside. This is unusual, an inmate left alone in a warden's office. But then, I wasn't really an inmate anymore, was I? Maybe he was just giving me my first taste of what it's like to be a free citizen. Or maybe he was hoping I'd steal something so they could lay a new beef on me. I looked around the office. It was full of prison art: crosses woven from sock threads, hollow men made out of toilet-paper tubes, soap sculptures. A toilet-papier-mâché mobile of a flying dinosaur, pterodactyl, made by yours truly, was suspended from the ceiling by dental floss, and I felt like cutting it free and taking it with me. That would be cold: getting sent back to prison for stealing a piece of your own prison art.

What I did was sneak a peek at my psychological evaluation, as prepared by the chief shrink. My jacket—my file—was sitting right there on the warden's desk. In addition to saying I was refractory, it said I had become completely "prisonized"— been in the Life so long I only knew and understood the customs and mores of the joint. "Inmate Brock's reentry and adjustment to the outside will present a greater challenge for him than it does for most younger inmates," he wrote. "This is especially true in consideration of his NKRC classification."

The warden came back in. "So any thoughts about the future, Dwayne?" He was nothing if not persistent.

"Tourism," I said. "I've got experience in that."

For years I worked in a bullpen behind prison industries, answering phones on behalf of the New Mexico Department of Tourism. (You'd be surprised at the variety of jobs we had here—it wasn't just banging out license plates.) The guys in the cubicles next to mine worked phones for Game and Fish, issuing hunting and fishing licenses, until some newspaper found out about it and raised a shit storm, saying now cons would know the names and addresses of people who hunted and therefore had guns at home. (As if that same newspaper hadn't reported that there are more than two hundred million guns floating around out there; getting hold of a firearm in America ain't exactly like breaking into Fort Knox.) So the governor closed down the operation, and as an afterthought he decided it'd be cute to have us dress in stripes and break rocks with sledgehammers, like in the old days. He went so far as to have the rocks shipped in—you can see the pile of them over in the main line—but the warden wisely ignored the plan.

I fielded calls from folks all over the country, all over the world. New Mexico's a big tourist destination. No, you don't need a visa to visit New Mexico, I'd tell them, it's a state of the

USA. Yes, there have been three cases of bubonic plague this year in the region, but that hardly makes it an epidemic. Just don't handle sick rodents—definitely drop any rodent handling from your plans. No, the Red Indians are fully contained, there is no danger in traveling after dark (that was to a woman calling from Ireland). No, I can't make the hotel reservation for you, you'll have to call them yourself.

My cellie laughed at my imitations of the callers and said I was a good actor.

"Or movies," I said to Warden Johnson. "Don't you think I'd be good in the role of an ex-con?" I knew about the plans to lease Old Main to the movie people.

The warden looked at me like I was a wise ass. But I meant it.

"As soon as they start filming here I could come up and see if I can get a role," I said.

The warden leafed through my jacket. I knew he was thinking, *This poor bastard can't keep from coming back, even if it's to play the role of an old con. He's prisonized for sure.*

That cellmate, young guy, thought I was a good actor but a dumbshit for not pretending to take the hotel reservations and therefore getting callers' credit-card numbers. I could act, he said, so why didn't I bullshit them?

"What would I do with those numbers?" I said. "They don't take credit at the prison canteen."

"Well, Brock, believe it or not, some of us are actually aiming to get out of this joint, and we might like some credit on the outside, so you could sell it to us. Anyways, you should know about these scams. I'll teach you. All the good scams these days involve information. This is the Information Age, if you hadn't heard."

He was a new fish, pink, but styling big.

"Do I look like a grifter to you? I'm a second-story cat man. Touch my ear."

He didn't want to touch my cauliflower ear, but I insisted, and like everybody he was surprised at how tough it is, pure cartilage.

"Listen," I said, and I made my nose click, that loud snap I can make it do when I pull it out of its leftward swerve. "You think with a mug like this I make a good flimflam man?"

"Nobody has to see your face or hear your nose, you operate over the phone or over the computer, but if that's the way you feel about it."

"That's the way I feel about it. I'm a second-story man."

When the warden was done with me, I handed one copy of my release form to the block officer, one to the guard at the sally port, and one to the bus driver. The fourth copy was for me. Two parolees and I got on the bus. We drove over the booby pit, where a hack checked to see if there were any escapees snuggled in the axles, and then we headed between the glinting razor-wire tunnels of the outer perimeter and were on our way to Albuquerque. These two parolees had kin in Albuquerque, and though they knew I was NKRC, they didn't invite me to meet their people, and who could blame them? They wanted to leave prison behind, and I was a walking reminder of it.

The clothes I was wearing were the same ones I'd worn the day I turned myself in for my last bitch, the big bitch: whipcords, snap shirt with smile pockets, thin leather vest, and a mean-looking pair of alligator boots with the toes curled up. They'd been all that time in Property, surviving fires, floods, riots, and various prison administrations. They had a cold, stored smell, and the boot leather was dry and cracked.

I had the driver drop me off at the Greyhound station—not that I was leaving town, but you always want to turn the Man around. It was still early, nine o'clock by the clock on the Wells Fargo bank building, but the desert sun was already hot and high. It smacked me like what they call a fill light on a movie set. I stood against the white wall of the depot, under the picture of the running dog, letting the sun blaze the prison cold off me. I wiggled my toes in my boots. In the heat, the old leather became warm and supple.

A couple of hopheads rounded the corner, hustled up with their hands in their pockets, and asked me if I was "looking."

I knew this was the Outside, and that these were just two street hypes pushing dope. Nine o'clock in the morning, and already pinjabbers were out and about: Albuquerque's a toddlin' town. But I couldn't feature guys approaching me with hands in their pockets.

"I'm not looking, I'm going blind," I said, balancing my weight on the balls of my feet, ready for whoop-de-do. "How many a you are there?" This weirdness was to throw them off their guard. Yet I did feel like I was going blind. It was too bright out there, the kind of brightness you feel when they finally take you out of the Hole's blackout cell. It hurts. The hopheads looked at me wild and took off.

Near the depot, by the railroad tracks, was a cantina, the Madrid, already open for business. It was a relief to enter that dim, cool cavern, though it was a disappointment to see only men hugged up to the bar. I wasn't interested in talking to men. I did plenty of that in the joint. Mostly I just watched the barmaid, who was Spanish and blonde and someone you'd want to watch. A toothless old drunk bawled real tears when she cut him off. She grinned at me and called him a cab. I wanted to remain someone a pretty barmaid would grin at and not someone she'd cut off and call a cab for, so I decided to go easy on the brews.

I wasn't used to drinking anymore anyway. I was never keen on pruno, jailhouse brew, since it tastes as nasty as the kitchen scraps it's made from. Then I found out that some of the guys dribbled piss in it to get the fermentation started. It's easy to jump on the wagon after you hear that.

Though I tried to drink slow, the beer went to my head. I thought I'd better get something to eat, but the pickled pigs' knuckles behind the bar didn't look too appealing for breakfast. I headed out to look for a restaurant.

Some of you are probably wondering what a con like me does for money upon reentry. Besides my hundred dollars in gate money, I had a little saved up from answering phones for the tourism people, even though they paid me only pennies per hour. It adds up, year after year, if you don't spend it all on canteen. You can also sell your plasma at the prison clinic, though I never could feature that. There was something too weird about receiving state-provided nourishment and then turning around and selling your bodily products to the state. Some of the prisoners liked the idea, thought it was ironical. But it gave me the creeps.

So I had cash, what we call white money, though I had no idea how far it would go. It was brighter than ever on the streets. I guess I'd been walking those dim prison corridors for so long that I'd become permanently sensitive to outdoor light. I'd also forgotten how fast things moved out there. A kid whizzed by on a skateboard, almost clipped me, no apology. The backward cap on his head read, "Fuck Off." Cars charged me, horns blaring. In two minutes I experienced enough rudeness to keep any self-respecting con busy for a year in murderous payback. But this was the Outside, I reminded myself again. That car that almost smeared me, its driver yelling at me? I'd never see it again. And nobody was going to sidle up to me and say, "That driver that disrespected you? What are you going to do about it? Because if you're not gonna stand up for yourself, I want you to bend over for me and all my buddies here."

That young cellie I was telling you about, who had some schooling, explained it to me like this once: the joint is a closed system where everything circulates tightly, every molecule affecting every other, whereas the Outside was an open system where things flowed on and disappeared. In the joint, what goes around comes around. Outside, it just goes.

Women. They were circulating here everywhere, fearlessly so. A world half full of women? That was a world not half bad.

I stopped in front of a plate-glass window and watched a waitress. She was dressed in a uniform with a cap and a little apron, like waitresses of the olden days. Cute as she could be. To be served a real plate by a real waitress for a change, instead of having some con glop your slop onto your tray with his rubber-gloved hand! I looked up at the sign. It said, "Eat at Joe's." This was the place for me.

Now, I had no idea this was an ironical place. In my day, there were many establishments with names like this. "Eat at Joe's" meant just that: "Come eat at this place run by this guy Joe." Some places were called, more simply, "Eat" or "Joe's." These days any such name is ironical. I understand that now, especially after conversations I've had with the movie people. The other night some of the crew and me watched *Natural Born Killers* on video, and they explained to me that it was ironical from beginning to end, a kind of spoof. Practically everything's ironical these days, they said.

I guess the world must have turned ironical while I was away. Prison isn't ironical. Things are what they are there. Meals are especially serious affairs. The mess hall can be a tense place. It's where a lot of fights come down and where the races segregate themselves the strictest. Maybe it's an animal thing, I don't know. When I entered that restaurant and smelled the food smells, I tensed up. I didn't care for the two Indians at the counter turning in their stools and looking at me. The waitress gave me a funny look too. She sat me far away from everybody else, in a booth back by the kitchen.

She wasn't as pretty as she'd seemed through the window. She was a little cross-eyed, her mouth a little skewed—her bright lipstick seemed to have slightly missed its mark.

"I could eat a horse," I said, and smiled my jack-o'-lantern smile. "But I'll take the liver and onions."

"Oh, now *that's* original," she said, her shoulders falling. "Eat a horse, right." She made ugly eating noises, snorting through her nose. Then she walked away neighing. Neighing and whinnying like a horse.

Now, it never occurred to me she was a ding, though it should have, because the mission statement on the back of the menu read, "Eat at Joe's proudly serves as a supported employment job site for rehabilitation programs of the Albuquerque Guidance Center." (In other words, Uncle Sam gave the owner a tax break for hiring dings.) And it's not as though I hadn't encountered my share of them in the joint; there's usually a whole cellblock full of them—the ding wing. I guess what threw me was that here was a ding in a service position. How could I know they were now letting dings out into the general population, and giving them jobs to boot? How would I know a restaurant had a mission besides that of rustling up grub with a minimum of courtesy to the paying customer?

When she came with the liver and onions, I was willing to forget the neighing and all and try conversation again. Maybe I'd spooked her somehow, the way those hypes had spooked me at the bus station, and that's why she had broken out in assholes.

"You all right? Joe treating you good?"

"Who, now?"

"The big guy. Joe." I waved my hand at the sign.

"Oh, my sweet Lord." Her hand shot up to her mouth, covered her twisted lips. "Oh, he thinks . . . Oh, you poor old thing."

She rushed back to the kitchen. I could hear her screechy voice: "He thinks a guy called Joe's the owner!" My grub tasted to me then like food loaf, that stuff they feed you in the Hole when you're hard-rocking: your whole meal ground up in a blender and baked in a loaf. I ate a few bites, threw money on the table, and left.

The code you learn to live by in the joint requires that you deal with an offense as soon as possible. If this waitress had been a man, you could be sure I'd have been in the kitchen immediately, tearing him a new one. But I was dealing with a woman here. This was unfamiliar to me. I wandered down the street in a sort of daze, tasting a sour taste of liver and beer.

I walked past a purple car. It started yelling at me.

"Stand back. Stand back. You have violated this vehicle's space. Protected by Viper."

I jumped back all right. I stared at that thing. It repeated its message. I almost laughed out loud. I knew exactly what it meant about its space. In the joint, you learn a lot about protecting your space. One of the first things you learn is to stay at least ten feet away from guards when you're talking to them, so that no one can accuse you of snitching. The other day, I heard a couple of camera guys struggling to get their shit up the stairway to the second tier, bitching about how tight the spaces are here. Just throw a couple thousand cons in a place like this and see how careful a man can get about keeping his tiny space and respecting that of others. That unapologetic kid on the skateboard? That waitress laughing in your face? Those people would be fucked.

Out here, a lousy purple car was wiser than the people. But I wasn't in the mood to humor it. I spun around and plunged my bootheel into its door panel, like a shot to the ribs. It started screaming like a son of a bitch. I could hear it blocks away.

I happened into an area I was actually familiar with: Old Town. Working in the tourism bull pen, I had told countless people how to get there and what they could find there. The old church. Galleries. Mexican restaurants out the wazoo. What I'd forgotten about was the fake shootout. So when I heard gunshots and shouting, my blood jumped. I thought it was the real thing, even though the shots sounded strangely flat. I saw a guy in a bandanna and spurred boots fall in the middle of the street. Tourists in crazy shorts stood licking ice creams and watching the guy writhe and die. Then I got it. I looked at the clock. Twelve. This was the reenactment of *High Noon* they held every Saturday! One of my all-time favorite films.

I wanted in. I just had to be in this. This was the release I needed. I ran over to the dead guy, dodging fire. I unbuckled his gun belt and yanked it off. He opened his eyes—*Hey, this isn't in the script!* But I knew I looked as bad as Eli Wallach or Clint Eastwood, badder, so he just shut his eyes again, preferring to think, *Well, maybe it is part of the show, and if not, I don't want to mess with this fucker.*

A fake train whistle blew. In the movie, everybody in town urged Gary Cooper, the sheriff, to catch that train and hightail it out of town before the bad guys rode in. Every once in a while the camera would cut to a clock. Tick tock.

The bad guys came swaggering up the street. A good guy emerged from behind the parapet of a roof. I let him have it. He fell like the stunt man he was. Another appeared around the corner and I got him, too. I took fire, but I dodged it.

I ran all over the set, plugging everybody. I didn't care if this wasn't in the script. I had my own script. My script said, *Kill 'em all, let God sort 'em out.* After a while, though, they stopped falling when they saw it was me shooting. They were on to me, knew I wasn't supposed to be there. I snuck up on one shitbird who was just standing by the side of the fake saloon trying to figure out what the fuck was going on—I'm good in the stealth department, I hadn't been a second-story cat bandit all my life for nothing—and let him have it. Those blanks are loud. This fucker jumped to high heaven and stumbled into the street, turning to stare at me, scared shitless.

A cocksucker in a big white hat started toward me. Everybody stopped shooting. He had a sheriff's badge on—he must've had Gary Cooper's role. This was the boss, the choreographer or director or whatever, come to relieve me of my part. He looked plenty pissed that I was ruining the show. He had his hand out. The hand said, "Now give us the gun back, sir." But when I took aim at him, he backed away fast, my good acting making him forget that the gun held only blanks.

I ducked behind the storefront prop, hiked up the gun belt, covered it with my untucked shirt, hopped a wall, snaked an alley, and then strolled leisurely and high-headed down Rio Grande Boulevard.

I remembered how in the movie Gary Cooper stuck it out in the town, even though everybody urged him to saddle up. He stood his ground; otherwise his humiliation would have lived with him forever. He had principles. Well, I had principles too. I knew what I had to do. I had to go back to Eat at Joe's and get squared with what had happened there.

I felt that my humiliation by that waitress would circulate

back to me forever unless I did something about it. I realize now that I was still prisonized and operating within what that ex-cellie of mine called the closed system. I've come to realize this after seeing how movies are made and how drastically different an actor can be in real life from the role he's playing. The *movie* is a closed system where everybody has to be in character and play their roles. It's hard to do. That's why they have to have directors and that's why it takes so many takes to get it right, because *reality* is messy, open, changeable, like those actors' real personalities. People don't go to movies to see reality but to enjoy the illusion of a closed system. In fact, there's probably people right now reading this thinking that this philosophizing doesn't sound like Brock the con, the second-story man, that it's "out of character" for him; they want the prisonized Brock, the refractory Brock, the Brock who can only think of one word beginning with *F*. The Brock who can't learn anything new and who keeps repeating the same mistakes. Well, I can certainly offer them the old Brock in the following scene, which is exactly how it happened in reality.

Eat at Joe's was full of the lunch crowd. The waitress was ringing a guy up, stabbing at the keys, her lips scrunched. I waited my turn politely. Then I lifted up my shirt just enough for her to see the holster.

"Just the cash, sweetheart. Don't make a peep."

Well, she made a peep. She screamed with all the power of her whacked-out soul. She bolted through the swinging aluminum doors of the kitchen: "HE'S GOT A GUN!" This was definitely not in the script, these were not the lines I had written for her. Her correct lines, to be delivered in a frightened whisper, were, "Okay, mister, okay. Look, I'm really sorry about being a smartass bitch earlier. Here's the money. Anything else? Do you want a blow job? Come in the back and I'll give you a blow job." Something like that.

People near the front door scrambled out to the street. The rest got under the tables. Albuquerque people know what to do in a holdup, it's practically a reflex. Except that crazy bitch, of course. I hammered at the cash register with the butt of the six-gun. The cashbox was one of those new—new to me, anyway—electronic kinds and I had no idea how to open it. I picked it up and whammed it to the floor. Its lights went out, but it stayed clammed. I stomped it. I kicked it. I felt like a little kid having a fit or an old fool being an old fool. I didn't like this role. I could feel the people under the tables watching me like I was the real ding there.

I backed out of Eat at Joe's slow and easy, without flashing the piece. I hiked down the street quickly, the ugliest word in the world pulsing in my brain: *botched.* A botched robbery. Bungled. Now I was shamed twice over.

Nobody did anything to stop me. I could practically hear their thoughts: *Just let the old fool go. Police'll get him sooner or later.*

I didn't stop until I got to a little park. I was hot and tired. There was shade there, and deep green grass. It had been many years since I'd laid down on grass, under a tree. I told myself now was the time. There might never be another. I drifted off in that coolness. I awoke to three cops standing over me, the three eyes of their drawn Glocks staring down at me.

The Bernalillo County Detention Center was as familiar to me as the quiet park was unfamiliar: I knew its clanging noises, its rancid smells, its heat. The CO didn't need to tell me to bend over and spread my cheeks; I knew the routine. My thumbs were ready for the ink. I stood tall for my mugshot, making a crisp quarter-turn to give them a good view of that cauliflower ear and a profile of the crooked nose. The CO took my street clothes to Property. They'd enjoyed the light of the Outside for nearly eight hours.

"I could eat a horse," I said to the kid in front of me in the chow line.

"Yeah," he whispered. He looked dazed.

"What beef they lay on you?"

"What?"

The kid couldn't even talk. A first timer, pink fish. He wasn't hungry, either. I took his burrito.

I stayed awake most of that hot night, listening to the sounds. Snores, farts. The kid—another kid—on the bunk below, softly sobbing. A "No!" shouted down the tier, from a guy dreaming a nightmare, or living one. No, I can't say I liked jail, but it was familiar. I thought of what it would feel like to wake in the park, on the cold ground and under the faraway stars, an NKRC with nowhere to go.

A few days later, while I was slapping dominoes with some Cubans, I got a call from Warden Johnson.

"Eight hours of freedom, Dwayne," he said. "A whole eight hours."

"Felt like a lifetime, Warden."

"The DA told me all about it. I told him you'd been a model prisoner, which as you know is an exaggeration. You know what he said, Dwayne? He said, 'Then I'm sure you'll be glad to have him back. Because he hasn't been much of a model on the Outside.' How could I argue with that, Dwayne?"

I agreed that that was hard to argue with.

The DA's office wanted to get me bitched as a habitual offender. Again. A habitual. They also thought up new charges in relation to the *High Noon* affair. Never mind that the gun carried blanks: they wanted to get me on being a felon in possession of a firearm. Then they tacked on a fraud beef for my having acted as if I was one of the actors. They wanted to get me for impersonating a bad guy!

"But guess what, Dwayne. There's a good guy in all this: the director of the picture they've begun filming up here, Roger Rudman. I happened to mention your case to him, and he came up with this idea. Since the DA thinks prison is the only place for you, and you apparently agree, but since John Q. Taxpayer is tired of footing the bill for your living here, Mr. Rudman suggested you could earn your keep as caretaker of Old Main. Keep an eye on the place while they're using it for movie sets. You'll belong to the union, get benefits, the works. And since you obviously have a flair for the dramatic, you might even get some bit parts."

Oh, that was irony in his voice!

"Anyway, I think the DA'll agree to it, as long as it goes down as a conviction. We'll call it custodial probation. Everybody's happy, okay? The DA's got his conviction, Rudman's helped a guy—he's a do-gooder like a lot of Hollywood people, and I hope you appreciate that—and I can technically say that a guy I set free didn't get sent back up after eight hours. And you, Dwayne, you'll be back home."

I didn't mind the warden calling Old Main my home, even if he said it ironically. Because that's what it is, home, every empty tier and wing of it. Everybody needs a home, it's only natural. Even a homeless guy has a home, though it might be just a spot under a bridge or a favorite chair in the bus depot. In con talk, your cell is your "house." A prisoner will invite another prisoner over to his house for coffee, all very formal, the guest sitting on the little round metal stool that's attached to the table while the host mixes instant crystals and sugar in plastic cups—one lump or two? And some of the worst words you can hear in the joint come from the shift commander when he's looking for contraband or escape routes or is just feeling vengeful: "Tear down this house," he tells his minions, and they do, with relish. If it's dope they're looking for, they'll throw in a skin search and finger wave, and the invasion of your person is complete.

Now the whole place is my castle, and I'll defend it as such, every cellblock and tower and yard of it. The movie people don't fear leaving any of their shit lying around. Nobody's going to fuck with it as long as I'm here.

So far, I haven't spent a single night inside. I've been throwing my bedroll smack in the middle of the rec yard, to really keep an eye on the set. I never realized how big the sky can be at two, three in the morning. There were many, many years during my incarceration when I never saw the night sky at all, not once. The closest I got to seeing stars was in the Hole—and there was a time when just picking your nose the wrong way got you the Hole—where it was so dark that the only entertainment you had was to poke your own eyes and watch the show: meteor showers, exploding supernovas. Sometimes I lie here and think of that past, of the old days in the joint, and I can hear a faint noise from the new facility, though I know it's just my imagination, because those few hours of the early morning are the only ones when the racket of a thousand TVs and radios and flushing toilets and yelling voices subsides. Then I try to think of the future that I could've had, that I might've had, on the Outside, but I can never get a handle on it. I can only feature myself waking up in some park under this same sky, some cop nudging me with his shoe, telling me to get a move on, find a shelter. That's as far as it gets. Maybe the fact that I can't get beyond that would satisfy that old chief psychologist, the one who said I was stuck in my ways, prisonized, unable to imagine better things. But again, he's wrong. Because as soon as I stop thinking about myself, or in order to stop thinking about myself, I start imagining the next day's scenes, how they might go, all the things that might happen on the set. You might say I'm getting movie-ized. *Roll it*, Roger Rudman's assistant says, and the scene comes alive. *Cut*, he says, and then I fall asleep.

No Moo Goo

I'D DONE ONE year at New Mexico State University, and already I was a smartass. I thought I knew everything. One of the things I knew was that I didn't want to spend the summer back in Clovis working at my parents' café. But I had to, said my father, and I had to get back to the restaurant quick, because we were overdue for the New Mexico Environment Department's inspection.

I barely had time to scour out the barbacoa tank before the inspector came. Nothing stinkier than the scum left from boiled mutton heads, and no worse job than to squat in there and scrub. But it would be looking for trouble to ask my father why he hadn't hired someone to do these things in my absence. I wasn't supposed to *be* absent; college to him was a waste of time and money—I was supposed to have been at the café all along, helping with the family business.

The inspector was a fat, pasty-skinned guy who my father said owed his girth to doughnut bribes he must be getting from the Do Not Stop, which always got perfect quality ratings. The Do Not Stop couldn't be all that clean, said my father, because one day he'd driven by and seen a jumbo gray rat scuttling out of its back door with an oozing jelly-filled in its jaws.

My father believed this inspector had it in for us. A couple of years before, the inspector had discovered we were using

105

wild trompillo berries to separate the curds from the whey in making our asadero cheese. Trompillo belonged to the nightshade family and was indeed poisonous in large doses, but you had to use it to make real asadero. The inspector, rearing his massive face back to assess my father, said he understood the plant was also used in Messican folk medicine as an abortifacient. He defined the word for my father, whereupon my father promised to stop making the cheese immediately; heaven forbid we'd become known as the Home of the Abortion Quesadilla.

Today the inspector produced a pair of latex gloves from his back pocket, then stretched and snapped them onto his thick hands. He swept a little brush under the refrigerator, gathering dust and dead bugs, including one very desiccated roach. He placed the roach delicately in a stoppered flask as if it were a valuable scientific specimen and settled the flask in a velvet-lined concavity inside a fancy box.

He checked the refrigerator's temperature with an instant thermometer and wrote the figure down in a black notebook. He scooped some masa harina from its bin and poured it into a little sieve and examined it for weevils and foreign matter. He did many things of this sort in the kitchen while my parents watched with hooded eyes.

Then he stepped out onto the patio, crushing beneath his boot an egg laid right smack on the threshold.

The chickens were a new thing, acquired by my parents while I was away at school. Our mexicano customers had remarked one time too many on the unappetizing pallor of our eggs—mexicanos liked their yolks deep yellow, the yellower the better—and my parents decided to do something about it. So they got their own chickens and fed them marigold petals, what my mother called zempasúchil. The resulting yolks were almost orange, like the rising sun on a hazy morning.

An egg laid on the threshold of the patio door would normally be a sign of good luck, but when the inspector turned up the sole of his two-tone boot and observed the shell-spangled goo, the disgust on his face told us nothing good would come of this. In the first place, you couldn't have barnyard animals, or any animal, running around an eating establishment, but before he could assert this, my father assured him that the patio was not currently open to dining. "Be that as it may," said the inspector, to whose fancy language I was alert, "the yolk of this egg is inordinately yellow."

My father explained to him about the marigolds. He showed him the new slogan on the breakfast side of our menu—*nuestros blanquillos son más amarillos*—and tried to interpret the play on words.

"You know eggs, that's a very bad word in Spanish. Means, you know—" he lowered his voice—"the balls. So when we're being polite, we call them instead the little white ones. Blanquillos. So here we say, 'our little white ones are more yellower. Yellow.' I'm thinking if the restaurant was over in Amarillo we could say, 'we have the yellowest little white ones in Yellow.'"

My father was babbling, the way he did when he was stressed. The inspector regarded him with unsympathetic, watery-gray eyes. Then the man produced a curious little brushed-aluminum case from his tool kit. Inside the case were two foam-lined spaces. He took a pair of eggs (conspicuously not as clean as commercial ones) from our refrigerator and placed them in these spaces, closed the elegant case, and put it back in his kit.

The implication enraged my father, though he didn't show it until after the man had left. Another man taking his huevos— precisely two of them! The insult was patent.

"In México, a man could get killed for a stunt like that!" he bellowed.

"Pero no estamos en México, Fructuoso, and this is his job, to collect and analyze suspicious foods, and you know the gabachos don't like color any more than we like pale," said my mother.

We received a C rating for that reporting period, a blow duly reported on the local news. Nothing wrong was found with the eggs per se, but the chickens were deemed to be wandering too close to a food-serving area. And then there were the roaches under the refrigerator. My father blamed me for not being around that spring to help move the massive thing so we could clean under it.

"Why can't you transfer to the school over here?" he said, meaning, I hope, Portales, because no way was I going to go to the community college. "Then you could help out when you're needed. This is your patrimony!"

I tried to change the subject. "Did you know that an egg is a single cell? A single, huge cell. The yolk's the nucleus, the white is the cytoplasm. Freaky, no?"

"I don't know qué chingaos you're talking about, hijo. All I know is that when you're not here to help, the place goes downhill. We got a C!"

"Peking Palace got a C," I said, realizing as soon as I said it that I'd opened up a sore subject: the Asian invasion. The Peking Palace had been in Clovis forever, but recent years had seen the appearance of Thai and Vietnamese and Indian restaurants with names like Lotus Blossom and Taj Mahal and Lemon Grass Café. Those places, with their delightfully different uses of spices already familiar to the mexicano palate (cumin, chile, cilantro), their fragrant jasmine rice, their coconut-milk curries, their beautiful brown waitresses, charmed, and increasingly charmed away, our mexicano customers.

One Monday, when our own café was closed, he decided to take my mother and me to the Lotus Blossom so we could check out the competition for ourselves. We drove across town, the clouds on the horizon before us enormous stacks of gray stones with golden light spraying through their battlements. "Like castles," my father remarked.

"That's right, Papi!" I exclaimed. "Altocumulus castellanus."

"Altocumuloqué?" said my mother.

"Castles in the sky! Then there's cumulonimbus incus, the kind that looks like a big anvil, and cirrostratus fibratus, which is the kind that puts a halo around the moon and means a norther's coming, and altocumulus undulatus, which you guys call the cielo aborregado, and it really does look like sheep's wool—"

"Your home is your castle," my father interrupted. "Isn't that what they say?"

We got to the Lotus Blossom just as the castellanus began to grumble and crumble, its stones collapsing into a drenching rain.

The rain pounded the roof of the restaurant and my father noted with satisfaction how a waitress had to scurry around placing buckets under leaks. Meanwhile, a row of mexicanos enjoyed their pad thai and kung pao chicken and yellow curries, reaching for sriracha and soy sauce and sweating and laughing, unfazed by the leaks. They were mostly young guys, farm or ranch workers probably, and they all sat on a bench on one side of a long table, as if sitting across from one another were too intimate. Some kind of Asian rock, heavy on the cowbells, played on the jukebox until one of the mexicanos got up and punched in puras rancheras.

The waitress brought us our menus, each consisting of half a dozen tall, laminated sheets bound with golden cords and listing over two hundred numbered items to choose from.

"These menus or books?" my father said.

"Menu," said the waitress, oblivious to his sarcasm. She was very pretty, sloe-eyed and copper-skinned. She could have passed for a Chicana.

"Remarkable how phenotypically similar we are to the Asians," I said. "Living proof that our indio ancestors crossed the Bering Strait."

My parents once again ignored my pedantry. "Moo goo gai pan," said my father. "See there, number sixty-three? Do you think anybody orders the moo goo?"

"How does that raza know what anything is?" I said, eyeing the mexicanos at the long table. "I'm sure the waitress doesn't speak Spanish."

As if to answer my question, one of the mexicanos got up

from the table, cracked open the swinging door to the kitchen, and asked in Spanish what "esquid" meant. He didn't pronounce the "u," so it came out "eskid."

"¿Cómo, cómo?" came a voice.

"Esquid," he repeated, louder.

"Calamar, hermano," came the reply, over the banging of pots and pans.

"There you have it," said my father. "Just ask the cook. I bet every cook back there is mexicano."

"And every one them has learned to make moo goo," I said.

"No restaurant can run without raza anymore," said my mother.

"The problem is, they all tell their friends and relatives to come eat here," my father said.

The other problem was that the food was pretty damn good. We ordered a variety of delicacies (though not the moo goo gai pan), beginning with egg rolls, their spring-green bean sprouts visible through the translucent wrappers. Our restaurant's dishes, heavy on the meat and the masa, were peasanty by comparison. Even the main starch here, rice, had a delicate perfume. My mother remarked on it.

"Well, I could use a fajita plate," said my father. "At least you know what you're eating. Of course, fajita meat going up the way it is, pretty soon we won't be making any money off that."

My father's complaint about the rise in the price of flank steak, which I'd heard him make before, didn't make any sense to me. Sure, it had doubled in price in the last few years, but that was only because fajitas themselves had become so popular. Surely, I said, the rise in price was more than offset by the increased demand.

"Carambas, hijo, you know it all! The names of clouds, where indios come from, the economies of meat. What don't you know?"

"Economics," I said. "Not 'economies.'"

My father sat back in his chair and glared at me, stroking his moustache.

"Or economies," I said quickly. "Same thing."

"Since you already know it all," he said, "why keep going to school? Come back to us and contribute to your patrimonio. If you had been here you could have helped move the refrigerator and we would have found that roach."

My mother nodded her agreement. So we were back to that again: me quitting school and returning home to help with the restaurant.

"If I stay," I said, "would you let me revamp the menu?"

"Revamp? What's that?" my father said.

"Redo it. Add things to get back some of the customers we've lost. Or some new ones."

"Like what?"

"Moo goo?"

"No moo goo!" my father said with a laugh.

"Well, how about giving things a French twist? Huitlacoche crepes and foie gras flan?" I was half-serious, thinking of an upscale Mexican restaurant in Juárez a group of us from the dorms had ventured to one Sunday. *That* was the future: mexicano but different. It might work even here in Clovis.

"Qué foie ni qué las cucarachas," said my father. But I believed he'd let me try, if that meant I'd stay.

"Speaking of flan," I said, "some people cook it so long it tastes like scrambled eggs with syrup." My mother sometimes overcooked the flan like that, but I didn't want to say so directly and hurt her feelings.

"A proper flan," I went on, "when you make an incision on the top, should peel apart slowly, between a minute and a minute and a half from top to bottom." I'd made that up, but it sounded pretty good.

My father called for the check. I thought maybe he was afraid that if we tried the desserts, those mango and coconut concoctions the mexicanos were now devouring, we might declare them more delicious than our homely desserts of quince paste and crystallized fruit and too-dry lemon cake.

"For kicks, maybe we could offer some pre-Columbian

selections," I said. "Roasted grasshoppers and maguey worms. Imagine all the grasshoppers we could harvest from our backyard."

"Imagine," my father said.

It was dark when we left the Lotus Blossom. The storm had passed but the ozone-charged wind remained, so strong and steady that the traffic lights stretched facedown, shining green and yellow and red on the wet pavement of the streets of Clovis. I felt pleasantly and powerfully full of curry and rice, but those lights bothered me, ducking their heads like that, as if refusing to face me directly with any signal that might help me decide the course my life should take.

My Dealer, In Memoriam

I'M TALKING ABOUT heat, hard, blue afternoon heat, but I get a bone chill when I see that *he's not here.* So what do I call him? *You cocksucking son of a*—but why? What has he done to deserve this? He's just not here. Here at home, his home. Is it a crime not to be at your home?

So there is no need to cuss him. No need at all. Don't even think unkind thoughts about him. Let him come home. Come home, Rick.

Nor is it a crime to hang out on the sidewalk waiting for him. By the bleeding tree. The tree has a big wet spot on its trunk from a place where a limb was lost. The bark has closed over the wound like a pair of fat labia. A tree pussy. It smells cool and dank, like my spot under the bridge. I bury my face in it and breathe in the dankness.

Rick's dog thinks it's a crime for me to be out here. If I get any closer to the house, he goes apeshit. I've seen what he's done to the inside of that door. One day he's going to gnash his way through it and chomp someone's ass: someone like me.

He's much too smart, this dog Jerry Garcia, to lick up anti-freeze or a spiked meatball. Chocolate'll explode a dog's heart, but he'll no doubt avoid that too. To silence him, you'd have to shoot him, and gunfire has a nasty way of waking the neighbors. Jerry Garcia is definitely the best protection Rick could have for his stash.

I put my tongue to the cool moisture coming out of the trunk. Lick tree pussy. Maybe no one has ever said those words in that order before. Lick tree pussy. This is a first! Cool tree pussy.

My mind races with inane thoughts like these whenever I have to wait for Rick. Later, when I've got my bags—he's going to have to front me the dope, I'm completely broke right now—and I'm under the bridge, cooking my spoon, my mind will relax and empty. What goes up must come down. I like going down. Down, down, down into the endless end-lit tunnels and interlocking chambers.

Not Rick! Rick is an upper kind of guy. The powders he personally likes glisten: crystals and snow. My powders are a dull, dirty white, tinged with yellow. He keeps his crystals in glass vials. My powders come in cute little heat-sealed bags embossed with names like DOA and Kryptonite. He stashes them in a children's lunch box plastered with pictures of the gluttonous Taz, teeth bared.

Where the hell is he?

I'm sucking tree pussy when I hear quick footsteps on the sidewalk. Rick! I turn, wipe damp bark crumbs from my mouth. Jerry Garcia sets up another ruckus.

Quick steps like Rick's, but it's not Rick. It's this guy Paolo, who stops and stares at me.

"What," I say.

"Get outta here," he says.

He's some kind of hybrid type, red kinky hair, freckled brown skin, yellow eyes. His family must be either very rich or very poor. And he's a tweeker, like Rick. Tweekers have contempt for me and my dingy powders. We're different animals. They don't sleep. And they think that's all my powders are good for, to make you sleep. One time when we're both over at Rick's, scoring, Rick says about me, "This dude likes the nod. But we'll sleep when we die, right?" and Paolo imitates me nodding off and laughs.

"Fuck you," I say to Paolo now. "Where's Rick?"

"Rick's dead."

"Bullshit."

He sees I'm not going anywhere, and he gets another idea. "Help me clean up the place before the family gets here."

The family? Somehow these words make me believe him now about something bad happening to Rick. *The family.*

"You distract the dog," he says. "I'll go in the back."

I understand what he's up to. He's going to save the family the grief of finding Rick's stash. Of knowing about that part of dear Rick's life. This is very kind of Paolo.

Jerry Garcia's bashing his muscular body against the front door. If I stand here he'll keep doing that and won't hear Paolo go through the bedroom window.

It's not much of a door. It's hollow—I can tell by the sound as Jerry hurls himself against it. Paolo climbs through the back window and Jerry hears him. Jerry's very emotional but he has a sharp sense of reason, too, and though I rattle the door to keep him where he is, he decides a man actually inside the house is worse, and he takes off down the hall. Paolo manages to slam the bedroom door in Jerry's jaws, just in time.

Jerry's wild with rage. He returns to the front door and hurls himself over and over at it, and can you believe it? He breaks it down, he breaks through somehow, and then I'm running running running running to that pussy tree and bounding up it like the primate I am, leaving one huarache below for Jerry to rip to shreds. Lights come on in the house across the street.

Paolo climbs out the window. He's got the child's lunch pail: it glints in the moonlight. Jerry takes off after him, but Paolo's gone, on fleet tweeker feet. I scramble down the tree and take off the other way.

I know where to find Paolo: Starbucks. As if their crank isn't stimulation enough, these meth heads crave caffeine and sugar. He's sitting in his open Jeep in the parking lot, licking the cream off a mocha. I sneak up and jump in next to him.

Hot coffee sloshes over his hand. "Holy shit!" He grits his

teeth. "Mother*fucker*." But he doesn't want to mess with me, so he reaches into the back seat for the lunch box.

Inside lie nine tiny glassine bags of DOA. I wonder if he's holding out on me, but I'll take what I can get. I don't ask him how Rick died.

I hustle down to my bridge, remove a stone from its arch. That's where my rig rests, in that little crypt. I cook up, tie off, glide into the endless green chambers . . .

Three days later, eternity ends. I awaken to a morning jogger thumping over the bridge, seeking his endorphin high. Fatty breakfast smells mix into the haze hanging over the river. Coffee. Whoosh of a motel toilet: someone just enjoyed a lovely morning crap.

People awakening to their own addictions and pleasures.

I know it's been three days because each bag lasts about eight hours, and I've run out of bags. It's going to be another hot day; I can already feel the prickle of the heat, a trickling of sweat, but the prickling that actually awakens my sense of dread comes from within. It maps my skin, my nerves, my veins, my bones, like those pictures on transparent sheets in anatomy books, those superimposed graphics that you peel away to view the muscular system, nervous, circulatory, skeletal. My parents gave me such a book the year I kept insisting that I wanted to be a doctor when I grew up. I loved peeling the pages away, hearing that shearing sound as successive layers of the human organism revealed themselves. In a few hours, if I don't score another bag, I'll feel my body as those pages, a child's grubby hands tearing my skin from my muscles from my veins from my nerves from my skeleton.

Rick. Is Rick really dead? Paolo's slimy enough to make up something like that to get me to help him rip off Rick's stash. But when he mentioned the family—*help me clean up the place before the family gets here*—I believed him. I still believe him. Because who among us talks about families, our own or each other's? It just isn't done.

The public library is where I go to cool off and get my head together. In the restroom, I splash cold water on my face, suck it into my mouth. It stinks in there, beyond what a bathroom should stink. To prevent people from shooting up or indulging in other devilry in private, there are no doors on the stalls. In the first stall sits a heavy grunter, blinking with slow pleasure the way my cat used to when she laid a turd. I myself haven't shit since before my nine-bag run. I will soon enough, though, and it's going to be a fine old brick.

I flop down in one of the sagging armchairs in the periodicals room. I once read about heroin and morphine and all the opiates, sitting in this very chair. The article said those narcotics in their pure form harm no organ of the body. They found this old doctor dead of natural causes, and then discovered that he'd been shooting up morphine for fifty years. Never had a single malpractice suit, either. Good for him—he had a steady supply. Like me with Rick, until now.

Only problem is, you get hooked. And only the jonesing addict knows what true suffering is. The jogger gets irritated when he doesn't get his exercise, the fat man frets when he misses his sausage, but this is nothing compared to that tearing of the pages of your anatomy and the feeling that a barbed wire is being drawn through every one of your veins. The explanation goes like this, according to my reading: when you get addicted, your body forgets how to produce its own natural endorphins, and when your powders wear off, it stands churlishly aside like a cheated-on wife and says, "You feel bad? Go to your lover," knowing that your lover no longer thrills you like at the beginning of the affair but is now necessary to palliate the pain of separation of you from your body.

I'm going to have to start panhandling to scrape up enough change to score whatever filthy, stepped-on shit I can find on the street. But for now I watch a cadaverous old man take the local paper, bound in its primitive split-wood holder, from the hanger, and it dawns on me that the papers might have news about Rick's death, if it's true he's dead. I scour the last few days' issues. Nothing. The old man with today's paper nods off, the paper collapsing gently into his lap. I sneak over, tug it from his gnarled paws.

"Hey!" he shouts, but I'm off. I take it to a secluded carrel upstairs, peruse, and there, in the obits: Richard Calvin Montrose.

Richard Calvin Montrose? That you, bro? The picture looks like it's from a high school yearbook. *Dude, what happened?* (I don't know exactly what I mean by this. Do I mean what happened to make you what you were then, or what happened to make you what you became?)

The obituary starts off, "Richard Calvin Montrose, 22, loving son and brother, died unexpectedly last Tuesday." Toward the end it reads, "Rick had gone through some difficult times in recent years, but he was making progress on his dream of entering medical school and becoming a physician." I could see it: Dr. Richard Calvin Montrose, bopping around a hospital, checking patients, joking with nurses, raiding cabinets for pills. Rick, like me when I was a child, had wanted to become a doctor!

"A memorial service will take place Saturday. . . ." That's today. "At noon . . ." That's in two hours. "At First United Methodist Church . . ." Right down the street here.

The obituary makes me forget my pain for a moment. That is, it focuses me in the direction of loving my pain, because my pain means I'm still alive.

The cadaverous old man finds me. "Give me my paper, you son of a bitch."

I surrender the paper to his veiny hands. Why are these old fuckers so interested in the news? Do they think they can do anything about what's going on? Maybe they're just into the obits, like me.

"Spare change?" I ask in front of the library. Some derelict intellectual I've seen around before, a stack of books under his arm, wants to know what I mean, exactly, by "spare change."

"When, sir," he says, "is money ever 'spare'? Is it not the Substance Absolute? Or do you mean, 'do you have change you can spare?' Maybe you should say 'share' instead of 'spare.' Perhaps this would best preserve the truth of the matter. In any event, here." He gives me a nickel and four pennies.

I move down the street from the library, where there are fewer whacks but more, unfortunately, lawyers, since this is where the public defenders have their offices. The PDs are frankly sick of people like me and feel they are doing plenty for us already by representing us in court, so I keep moving on until I find myself in front of the church.

The service is already in progress when I duck in. The priest, preacher, pastor, or whatever he'd be called in this church, is speaking. The immediate family, or who I assume is the immediate family, is in the front row: mother, father, and who I later learn is Rick's sister, a small, dark-haired girl, twentyish. A smattering of other friends and relatives are in the pews behind. Aware of my body stink, I sit in the far back.

The priest talks about Rick's having gone to "a better place" and his "real home." All those kinds of platitudes that nobody really believes, or maybe they do. Rick himself didn't. I remember him once going on and on about how we're just chemicals. "Just a bunch of chemicals expressing themselves," is how he put it, as my insides literally itched for him to shut up and fetch the lunch box containing the chemicals I needed, and me thinking, *What kind of chemicals are going on in his brain to want him to torture me like this by keeping me waiting?*

But this is the priest's job, to say these banalities. A regular working afternoon for him, as for most people, whom I can hear, through the church's open doors, zooming back to their offices from lunch. Even Rick worked—dealing is work too. I'm the oddity who's never had a job, which I guess is part of the reason for my family's disgust with me. When my father died and left us the money, I didn't sock my share away and go out and get a regular job, the way my brother did. I sent it straight to my brain's pleasure center, via dope. I was spoiled, spoiled rotten, they all said, especially after they sent me to the fancy rehab place and it didn't take. All that I could expect from them now was tough love, which meant, basically, them writing me off. I wonder if they would take the time to come to my funeral, like Rick's people did for his, or would they keep tough loving?

I gaze at Jesus on the cross, above the altar. Tough guy. He's just hanging there, not screaming or anything. You never see him on the cross screaming. His natural endorphins must have kicked in pretty soon, zoned him out—maybe already kicked in as he was carrying the heavy cross and getting whipped and all. Of course, if he's God, would he really feel pain? Or would he feel *extra* pain? I never got religion: more questions than it answers. Too bad, because belief, true belief, must release all kinds of soothing chemicals. As Rick once said, making fun of Jesus freaks: "I used to be all messed up on drugs. Now I'm all messed up on Jesus!"

Again my mind's racing, as it does when I'm getting the grips and trying to repress my own agony. The preacher ends his requiem by telling us we'll all meet Ricky in heaven, and I can only think, *Will he have some bags for me there? DOA, say?*

And then something happens to distract me: Rick's sister, the petite, dark-haired one sitting up front, takes the stage. And I do mean stage, because what she has for us is a slideshow, accompanied by music—the Grateful Dead's "Death Don't Have No Mercy," from the *Live/Dead* album. The late, great Pigpen on vocals. This is amazing. Ricky was no Deadhead—he'd named his pit bull Jerry Garcia as a joke. She chose the music because *she* liked it. *I* like it: Pigpen's spooky organ and Garcia's space-guitar notes—Garcia was a smackhead too, the world now knows. This is different from the serious-celebratory sort of music you're supposed to have at these things, and I like that, too. All the pictures are of Ricky, of course: baby Ricky in the tub, little Ricky climbing a tree, big Ricky graduating from high school. People sob, the sister blows her nose, and I'm suddenly filled with oxytocin warm fuzzies. Oxytocin, the naturally occurring bonding chemical. I love these people. I love the sister, especially. I'm also thinking, *Judging from her taste in music, maybe she has some of my kind of dope she'd like to share? Even a joint would help.*

My rush fizzles when I see a guy with frizzy red hair pop into the side entrance of the church just as the service is ending. Paolo. Good timing, as always: he gets to the sister before anyone else, takes both her hands in his, starts on his own platitudes, one of which he says loudly enough for everyone to hear: "Okay, so he was only twenty-two, but he lived four years for every one of ours, so that made him eighty-eight, way beyond the average life expectancy!"

Really sorry about Ricky, I say.

"How did you know him?" she asks me, smiling wanly, but distracted, her wet eyes wandering beyond me.

"High school," I say. I add, "I was also planning to go on to medical school."

Paolo gives a snort.

I'm thinking that the sister, Amy, doesn't much like Paolo. But she invites us both to the gathering at the family home.

"I don't have a car," I say.

"Me neither," Paolo says boldly. I can see his red Jeep right out there in the church parking lot.

Amy tells us we can ride with her. Paolo commandeers the front seat, which is fine with funky-smelling me. I sit in the corner opposite of Amy and crack my window.

Amy seems lost in her thoughts and Paolo has enough sense to respect her silence, so I don't get to learn anything about how Ricky died, as I'd hoped. I watch the cars coming in the opposite direction and think, *One flick of her wrist, and that person there, or this next one here, who we otherwise will probably never see again, will become an intimate part of our lives—if we survive, anyway.* Sometimes I think this is how a lot of criminals think, which is why they don't mind getting caught, even *want* to get caught. The criminal's lonely. He needs family. The victim and the victim's family become his family. They become very intimate, their lives intertwined through court dates and newspaper reports and TV interviews. They learn all about each other. The killer apologizes, the family rebuffs the apology (though sometimes there's a renegade in the family who accepts it). They demand remorse, he seeks forgiveness. If it's a death-penalty case, the family gets the front seats at the execution. It's not just out of revenge that they go. It's out of the insatiable desire for intimacy. They want to enjoy the ultimate intimacy of killing the killer, just as the killer has enjoyed the intimacy of taking their loved one's life. It's only fair. It's only fair to killer and family alike to give them all this final experience of intimacy, of letting them watch him die.

We pull into the circular driveway of an hacienda-style home. Jerry Garcia comes tearing up, snarling.

"Ricky's dog," Amy says. "He doesn't seem to like you guys. Stay in here while I put him up."

While she's gone, Paolo and I don't talk. I scratch my arms, deep, long scratches. I wonder if he's having the same thoughts as I am: explore this family home, medicine cabinets first. . . .

The caterers drive up with the spread. She needs to tell them where to set up.

I say to her, "I really have to go to the bathroom."

"Me too," Paolo says.

"Down that hall and to the left," she says to me. "Down this hall, way in the back," she says to Paolo.

I cast him a *die, motherfucker* glance and hurry down my hall. It's true I have to go. Number two. It's time to lay my brick. You know how you're out all day, and then you come home, and suddenly you really have to go? Like that. Like coming home.

There are two doors to the bathroom, both of which I manage to lock just before I sit and let loose. It's not just one brick, it's a demolition, a whole junky building collapsed and spilling into the water. For that emptying moment, I forget my craving; but as soon as it's over, I'm reaching for the medicine cabinet. I scan its contents, zero in on an opaque bottle of what could be cough syrup, and, yes, it's the good stuff, with that lovely red warning on the side about drowsiness and heavy equipment.

The expiration date's come and gone and the top is glued shut with crust, and I wonder about lost potency as I marvel that anyone could let such a treasure sit around unimbibed for so long. I pour all of it into a toothpaste-smeared glass and top off the glass with water. Purple drank! I gulp it down and place the empty syrup bottle back in the cabinet. I examine the orange prescription bottles. All duds except one: Xanax bars! With the bottom of the glass I try to crush one of the long pills into a powder that I can snort, but the pill's hard and flies across the room, so I settle for swallowing three or five.

It's going to take a while for all this shit to take effect, but I'm calmer now just knowing it's in me. I sit on the edge of the tub and look around and realize the bathroom must be Amy's. Tampons, blush brush, eye shadow. Amy sent me to *her* bathroom! I'm suddenly ashamed of the way I've stunk it up, and of all my bodily odors. I spy a bottle of bubble bath in the corner of the tub and I think, *Do I dare?* I can feel the drank coming on, tingling my fingers and toes. I turn the ceramic faucet, and water gushes into the tub. I jug a big glug of bubble bath under the stream. The bubbles grow and peak. I peel off my sticky clothes.

The water's up to my ears; I hear ocean. How many bars did I down? The fragrant bubbles rise monstrously before my eyes, and I remember something about our universe being perhaps just one bubble in a frothy sea of universes, some moving forward in time, others backward. I continue my slow sinking. I breathe in the universes. I choke, choke so hard that bile rises up in me, and I choke on that too. My throat and lungs burn. I can't get air. *This has happened to better people,* I remember thinking, *Janis, Jimi.*

And, finally, a pounding at the door. Her alarmed voice, and the three silliest, most beautiful words in all eternity, in all those universes: "Are you okay?"

Judge, Your Honor, Sir

JUDGE, YOUR HONOR, sir, soon as you're booked you got to post bond and get the hell out of here. You know that, don't you? Sure you're in shock, everybody is, I mean, a judge, a *sitting* judge, swept up in a raid on a crack house and now in holding at the county detention center—man, the cops don't know whether to shit or go blind.

You remember me, don't you, Judge? Been before you many a time. I'm also one of the guys from the back of the bus, the 66. Recognize me now?

Say, Judge, did you really spark a rock? Is that why you're just sitting there, like embalmed? It'll do that to you. That's why I never touch the shit, myself. So, how about it—did you?

All right. You don't have to answer that. No jailhouse confessions required here. Stay clammed up. Be embalmed. But with all due respect, Your Honor, don't think you're so fucking special. You're not the first big taco ever caught sucking fumes. There was that mayor of Washington, remember? Big time crackhead. And let me clue you in on something else, Your Honor. Call me a tweeker, speed freak, or whatever, but I'm here to tell you crank delivers what coke only promises. Breakfast of champions. Crank makes you lucid, not stupid. I'm lucid, am I not? Am I not in control? And my voice is low, right? I'm not all overamped and yelling, "Hey, check it out, we got a real live judge in here, Judge Haskill!" No. I'm thinking clear, I'm in the zone. I'm tooling. So while we're sitting here, me thinking clear and you listening, let's talk strategy.

Judge, first and foremost you gotta go for the sympathy. All high-class defendants charged with low-class crimes play this card. It's only natural. An Albuquerque Metro Court judge popped with dope? He's no criminal—he's got personal problems. Nobody wants to hear the personal problems of us riff-raff. But yours, Judge? The problems that brought you so low? We're all ears.

Just tell the court what you told us on the bus yesterday. About how you hit the skids after your old lady dumped you. It's the oldest story in the book, and judges don't want to hear it from folks like me, but from you, a fellow judge? (A judge standing before a judge, a lawyer at his side! It's a weird thing to picture.) Because the judge judging you will be all, *There but for the grace of God go I.*

Tell it the exact same way you told us, except this time, sober! Tell it quiet, without getting worked up, which was how that argument with your old lady went the night she left you, right, you being high-class people? Not even an argument, just statements? Her statement: "I can't live like this anymore." (Live with you, is what she meant.) Your statement: "I can't make you." That was a piss-poor answer, Judge, you gotta admit. Sure, it's true. You can't make them. But the way you said it, just matter of fact like that, so unemotional. I mean, with all due respect, wouldn't it have been better if you'd dick-slapped her? Seriously, you sure you didn't say, "I have no jurisdiction over you in this matter"? Face it, that's what she hated about you, that cold, matter-of-fact, judgely way of yours. Nobody could ever get to you.

This control deal is what made you a good judge, though, in my humble opinion. I've been in a few courtrooms, including yours. (Sure you don't remember me? Theodore Lee James III, AKA Tweety?) I've been before tough-guy judges, nice-guy judges, jokey judges, sourpuss judges, sarcastic judges, the works. Here's what that fucking Judge Marlowe said to me last time I got arraigned before him: "Why, if it's not Mr. James again. He's so eager to get back into that prison jumpsuit he must think it has Tommy Hilfiger written all over it!" What a card.

You were different. (Not were—are! You're still a judge, you haven't been de-benched, yet—innocent until proven guilty!) You didn't fuck around. You were just a plain, cold hard-ass. Remember how hard you came down on us when we took clothes from the Goodwill bins? Not even inside the bins, just lying out there, donations! With all due respect, Your Honor— what an asswipe! Who did you think those clothes were for, if not for people like us? You were also the judge who refused to lower bonds, even though it meant jail overcrowding and more headaches for the white shirts. Look how crowded this fucking place is, Your Honor. Now you get to sweat awhile in the conditions you helped create.

Maybe you'll have a little more sympathy when this is all over, you think?

In your courtroom you created machine vibes. Machine vibes happen when everything proceeds smoothly—defendants are processed like sausages, one after the other. No joking, no flexibility, everything by the book. I'm wondering, Your Honor: Were those the vibes you created at home, too? Machine vibes? Were you, like, Mr. Efficiency there too? A real square john, a man with rules, a control freak? Your home a courtroom? Your kids just products to be processed according to the rules? Is that why they never come home to visit anymore, because they don't, do they? Is that why your old lady bailed, no pun intended?

I remember the day you fined yourself for coming late to court. I was there on a motion to dismiss, the first name on the morning docket. "Haskill's never late," my PD mumbled, who for the first time wasn't late herself. Then you walked in, sweating, buttoning your robe. You said "on the record," and the reporter took her seat, and you announced that you were fining yourself fifty dollars for getting to court late. You went on and on, making quite the case against tardiness, for responsibility, and so forth. I especially remember one thing you said: "I let the time get away. I wasn't policing myself, so I'm late." At first I thought you said, "I wasn't pleasing myself," and I didn't get it, because all the times I've ever been late it's because I *had* stopped to please myself, whatever that might mean—chase a dragon, get a blow job, whatever. But then you went on about how a guy's got to police himself, and this time I heard you right. What you were saying was, *A guy has to be his own cop!* Excuse me, Your Honor, but that is a ball-freezing concept right there. I thought, man, this guy's nuts. I figured you were going to decide then that a fine wasn't enough, you were gonna handcuff yourself and have your bailiff take you away to do hard time. My PD, meanwhile, is rolling her eyes, your clerk's looking at the floor all fake-serious, and the prisoners, well, we're just staring at you in amazement. I'm only being honest when I say that we all of us in that courtroom hated your guts at that moment.

The media ate it up, though. The judge who finds himself in contempt of his own court! A real man-bites-dog story for them. And a PR coup for you. Too bad you didn't need it; you weren't even running for reelection or anything. My question to you: At home, were you the kind of guy who fines his children for being late or not doing what they're told? Don't tell me: Were you the kind of guy that keeps score of his wife's fuckups? A kind of family rap sheet? Okay, I'll get off your case about it, if you'll stop staring at me like that. You know what you look like? Like a junkie staring at his candy man, desperate to hear what I'm gonna say but scared to know.

Don't peek out the window now, Judge, but talk about the media, they're all there. You don't want to face those cameras? But they've always been your friends, and the public likes you—you're what everyone expects in a judge. Just walk straight to them. I know you know that's what you should do. I know that's why you won't call your lawyer to help you on this thing: you think it's cowardly to hide behind an intermediary—you know that as a judge, a public servant, a *high* public servant (no pun intended), you should face your public directly.

My advice: tell them it's all a mistake and that you'll issue a statement later. That's as much as you have to say. Just a mistake—you're not saying your mistake or whose mistake, that's the beauty of it. "It's all a big mistake." Who could argue? I don't believe in evil. Do you? When bad shit happens, there's been a mistake somewhere along the line. A kid lops his folks' heads off with a machete, well, maybe they knocked him around too much. Their mistake. Or maybe he tripped and fell on his head as a baby and got wacky, but still a mistake. They should've been watching him, can't just blame his baby legs. Errors of judgment, right, Judge?

Later, if you decide to cop a guilty plea, you can come full clean, as you always asked us defendants to come with you. You can admit it was your mistake. A mistake to have been drinking yesterday. A mistake to have left home and ridden the bus. A mistake to have gotten off the bus with Horsy and them and gone to the Zodiac and then ended up somehow at Blind Chuck's with the crackheads.

Again, the beautiful thing is that people will want to know what happened in your life to bring you, a judge, so low, to make you make so many mistakes, do weird things like ride the city bus and hang out with us lowlifes. It will be established, as lawyers like to say, that at the heart of your case is your old lady walking out on you. At the heart, Your Honor! (Heart's a word one of my lawyers loved to use with a jury, touching his chest when he said it to remind the jurors to remember their hearts when deciding on me.) When she quit you, you started beating up on yourself about it, rattling around your big old house, all alone and lonely, asking yourself, *Why am I such an uptight asshole?*

That beating up on yourself lasted a couple of weeks—about two weeks, right? That's normal. You didn't sleep, you lost about ten pounds. People knew, and they noticed. *The poor son of a bitch*, they thought. You could hear it from their minds. It really got to you. Poor son of a bitch nothing, you said. I'm a fucking judge. I've got power. Nobody's gonna feel sorry for me.

So then you got tough. With yourself and everybody else. Take a look at your sentencings in that period and see if it's not true. You handed down all maximums for a while there. You revoked bond on all kinds of defendants, even after the white shirts at the jail complained that you were the main cause of the overcrowding. I heard it on the street. You told the chief judge to load up your calendar, told the cops they could call you any time of night to sign warrants. *You're not going to wake that bitch up anymore.* You didn't actually say it, but you thought it. It was the first time you'd ever called her something like that, even in your mind. It felt good, huh? Well, good and bad.

Your friends—which isn't that many, right?—were glad to see you busy. They thought that was the best thing for you, and they were relieved they didn't have to deal with you and your problems because they were plenty busy too. Busy folks: businessmen and politicians and whatnot. People you worked with at the courthouse knew what had happened, but no one was brave enough to approach you about it, except maybe a fellow judge or two, but you just blew them off, right? Like with your friends, you projected that you had your shit together, and they were happy to believe it.

A couple of months later, the depression hit you bad. Like in December? Christmas and all that shit. And it was a bitch of a winter, those cold winds whipping dust in from the Indian nations, day after day—I should know, I was living on the streets then. In January you got to court late twice, hungover, and those times there weren't no more perky speeches about policing yourself and all that. I wasn't in your courtroom either of those times, but again, I heard it on the streets. The word was you were actually back to bonding people out, you weren't being the hard-ass you'd been just a month before, you were too out of it, you were just going through the motions, splitting the bonds right down the middle: if the prosecutor asked for ten grand and the defense asked you to release the client on his own recognizance, you made it five. Automatically, without even listening to the arguments, your eyes half-closed. You looked like hell, they say, bags under your eyes, blood on your neck from razor nicks you hadn't noticed.

By February your hair was getting long and you were getting grease stains on your shirts, which you kept forgetting to take to the cleaners. You were still shaving, a man like you will always shave, shaving's the last thing you hang on to, never mind the nicks—hey, is that another thing that's freaking you out about having to meet the media, that you haven't shaved? We'll see if we can get you a razor. They stopped allowing them because guys were taking them apart and making little shanks by inserting the blades in the handles of their toothbrushes—but we'll find you something, when you're ready. Just say the word.

One morning in March, another windy, cold day, your car wouldn't start. You told Horsy this part, remember? You only had the one car—your wife had took the other. Which one did she leave you with? The Lexus, right? Well, you can't complain. It's normally a reliable vehicle, except that morning it wouldn't start. Just a click when you turned the key. Click. You sat there, grabbed the steering wheel. You wanted to put your fist through the windshield, but that's not something a judge does, that's the kind of thing the judged do, people given to emotional reactions, people who don't know how to police themselves. But is it fair to say you started to cry?

You just sat there for a while, in your cold Lexus, shaking, I mean sobbing. It's true, isn't it? You felt at the end of your rope, maybe you even imagined yourself swinging from the end of a rope. Or you imagined turning on the engine and filling the garage with fumes, except of course the engine wouldn't run, and even if it did, it's hard to poison yourself like that these days, what with emissions controls and all.

The tears were good for you, though. They washed you clean. You told yourself you could get it together. You told yourself to get out of the car, walk the two blocks to Central Avenue, and catch the bus to the courthouse.

Now, folks are going to wonder what made you think of the city bus instead of, say, a taxi. Let's face it, people of your stature, or status, or is it station, never consider the bus. It's a totally alien vehicle to people like you. The only time buses cross their minds is when they're in their way, and then they hate them and the people inside them. But you were more aware of the bus than most car people, from the things you heard in court. I remember that one activist lawyer giving you a little lecture on what it's like to be poor. A downward spiral, she called it, one thing leading to another. Her client was caught in that kind of spiral. Because his car broke down, he missed work and got fired. Without a job, he couldn't make the payments on the car, so he lost the car. Then, he couldn't get a job without a car. You listened with a little smile on your face, and when she was through, you said, "Counsel, can your client spell 'bus'?"

And I know more than one loser has stood before you mumbling that the reason he missed the appointment with his PO was because he missed the bus, and you're always hearing about cholo gangbangers encountering each other and throwing down at bus stops, and I believe you were the judge that sat on the case of that dim bulb Alpo, you remember, the guy who took the bus as his getaway vehicle, waited for it right outside the bank he just held up?

But the real reason you decided to take the bus is because you were beginning to get an attitude change. Am I right? For the first time in your life, you began to wonder what it was really like to be a loser. Oh, I'm not saying it was something hokey like you telling yourself, "I'm such a loser, let me go meet my loser people, the bus people." I'm not saying it was like a conscious decision. Just some instinct, that's all. So you wiped your eyes, got out of your car, walked to the bus stop two blocks away on Central, and waited for the 66.

I'd been up in the hills all night that night. You've heard of those party places where tweekers go up in the foothills, right? Cold in March, those nights, sure, but you build a big old bonfire. Man, there's nothing like watching a fire when you're amped, especially when it's windy. It's like watching your brain whipping in the wind. People were laughing, drinking forties, some of us slamming crank—you know what that means, don't you, like injecting meth? My legs felt like they were made of wire, like springs, and I started just jumping up and down in front of that fire, higher and higher, snatching at the stars. I thought I caught one; it burned my palm, and when I opened my hand it was still smoking. I thought it meant something. I didn't know what, but I had to find out, so I started walking, walking toward town, to the orange lights of Albuquerque. I could feel that hole smack in the middle of my palm, and it was telling me I was on my way to witness something important. I walked for probably hours, really trucking. By the time I got to Central, it was daylight, and the wind had died down, though it was still plenty cold. I had plateaued out, felt pretty smooth, but I still figured I was on some kind of mission. I caught the bus. Horsy and Pedro were sitting on the stretch-out in the back, nodding off. I was thirsty as hell and took a long pull from their warm forty while the driver was occupied taking tickets at the next stop. I'm screwing the cap back on and when I look up, guess who I see tottering down the aisle, unsteady as someone who's never been on a bus before, and maybe a little bit hungover too? Why, you, Your Honor.

Even though I'd never seen you out of your robes, I recognized you right off, and I knew you'd been blubbering, or had allergies, because of the dust and wind and all, but I figured crying. I'm pretty sharp when I'm on a plateau, if I say so myself, kind of like I am now. Clear. Controlled. I didn't go hollering to Horsy or Pedro, "Hey, check it out, it's Haskill, the judge!" And those juiceheads, they're so out of it, they didn't even notice. So I just watched you. You sat in one of the middle rows, kept your face to the window. We zoomed down Central, past the old Route 66 motels and the Zodiac Lounge, which maybe you've heard the cops refer to as the Star Wars Lounge because of all the extraterrestrial-looking weirdos who hang out there, and it was just opening its doors to let the early birds in. Horsy and Pedro, sensing we were close to those dives, woke up, made noises about getting off, realized none of us had a nickel, and went back to their boozy dreams. If they'd gotten off, I wouldn't have followed them; I had to make sure you got safely to your courthouse, Judge.

Donna got on around San Mateo. We bums were up and at 'em that morning, four of us now in the back of that bus. When we reached downtown, Donna pointed at the detention center and said, in that loud Oklahoma twang of hers, "Ain't it funny how all them people are in there because they don't *behave?*"

We all, all of us in the back, cracked up at this, just because of the way Donna said it, as though it had come to her as a major revelation.

"They just weren't *policing themselves,*" I said. The others didn't know where this phrase came from, they didn't know it was you who said it that time you got to court late, but it cracked them up again. I watched you sit up straight in your seat when you heard your words come back at you.

You started taking the bus every day then. We, the ones in the back, had piqued your curiosity. Every day you sat one seat closer to us. After a week, you were only two rows in front of us. Listening. Sometimes half-juiced, but always listening.

And thinking, right? Thinking about us losers and how we lived. People whose drivers' licenses you'd revoked, whom you'd jailed for public intoxication, for holding dope, people who couldn't get our acts together. Are you sure you didn't recognize me back there, Your Honor? The PDs used to call me a "frequent flyer," I was in court so much. One time you told me as I stood before you that I, and I'm quoting here, "seemed to be congenitally incapable of getting my act together and living like a responsible and productive citizen." I didn't have to ask what "congenitally" meant—I'm not that ignorant—I just thought, *This fucking judge, how the fuck would he know what I was born like? What the fuck does he know about me?* It pissed me off, Your Honor. But you know what? I saw that you were thinking the same thing when you sat on that bus, listening to us. I mean, you were thinking, *What do I know about these people I judge every day?* I sensed that's what you were thinking.

Yesterday was Saturday. You didn't have to go to work. There was only one reason for you to be on the bus: to be with us. You got on half-crocked, hell, shitfaced, that was obvious. Two-day beard. Donna had a snootful too, and when Horsy wouldn't give her a hit of his 20/20 she yelled at him, "Control freak freak *freak*!" Remember that? The driver had his eye on us. Horsy went up and sat next to you. Pedro calmed Donna down, giving her sips from his rum and coke. I sat in the seat behind you and Horsy. Horsy started asking you about yourself in that brotherly way of his, and that's when you spilled your guts about your wife and all, and I thought, *That's it, Judge, let it out. It's the road to recovery.*

Horsy gave you a big hug, and you needed that, didn't you? Because you hugged that brother in the dirty parka back hard, you sure did, I witnessed it. I saw your need. We all did.

I got off the bus in the middle of the hugging session, as you probably didn't notice. In a way I felt I'd accomplished my mission, that mission I'd embarked upon that day I came down from the party in the hills and found you on the bus, which was to see you become one of us, if only for a moment.

In retrospect to what happened later I know I should've stayed with you, Judge, to keep you out of trouble, but I had urgent business to take care of, business as it happened that got me popped last night too, just like you, but that's neither here nor there.

You guys got off at the Zodiac, that much I heard. I can see Horsy getting up and then turning to you and saying, "You comin'?" and those other two, Pedro and Donna, standing in the doors, holding them open, waiting for you, and the driver yelling, "Hurry up, let's go!" and you just following them into the street.

The sun was going down. If your old lady was still with you, you and her would've been on your patio with your martinis watching the sunset and the salmon steaks on the grill, your garden smelling sweet with all the spring flowers, grass all greened up, but instead you were following those folks into what you knew the cops call the War Zone, nothing green there just the bare-naked apartments ever since the cops butched down all the trees to keep dealers from hiding dope in the branches. Bombed as you were you must've been thinking, *Now I'm really slumming it.* How did that make you feel? Like you were experiencing the "real thing"? Or did you already feel yourself so much of this thing that you weren't looking at it like that, judging it, but just going with the flow of it, being a part of it?

How you guys ended up at Blind Chuck's is anybody's guess, though I suppose we'll find out in due course. I'm thinking it was Horsy's idea, right? That guy. He's acquired a taste for the rock, I'm afraid.

You all march into the darkness, no need to knock. "Come on in!" yells Chuck, after the fact, friendly like always. Dark, because why does a blind man need lights? Nobody can see you, so nobody recognizes you, not that they would have anyway, you looking so messed up. Blind Chuck offers you a warm beer—since he doesn't have electricity, he doesn't have a refrigerator. Folks are sparking bowls, just enough light to bounce off those shiny little knickknacks the crackheads give Chuck as gifts for letting them smoke at his place, all that little glittery shit they like to collect.

Horsy asks you for a twenty, you take some bills out in the dark, he lights a match to see the face on the bill—Andrew Jackson's face, horsy as his own—he talks to some shadows on the couch, a pipe or a redi-rock in a cigarette gets fired and passed around. I guess you probably figured by then you weren't gonna get out of there until all your bills were took and

135

all the rocks smoked. How much of that shit did you smoke? I bet not much, but I bet it took the top of your head off, being the first time and all. With all due respect, I wish I could've been there for that. I hope Chuck offered you some real liquor to smooth you out a little bit.

I don't know who brought the bust down, but I'll find out for you, I sure as hell will. I suspect Chuck's old lady just got tired of the party and called 911. She's done it before. Doesn't scream, doesn't fight—same as your old lady, Judge! Chuck's old lady just dials 911 and hangs up. The cops have to respond to all 911 hang-ups, you know that. The first time she pulled that stunt they didn't take her or Chuck into custody because they didn't want to mess with blind folks. They just cleared out all the crackheads, which is what she wanted. This time they took them both, her and Chuck, to the West Side jail with all the others, from what I understand. She shouldn't fuck with the Man like that.

But you know what, Judge? If I'd been there? I would've turned the Man around. I would've jumped right in and said, "Officers, we commend you for your ready response. This concludes Judge Haskill's undercover fact-finding investigation. Your supervisors will be receiving the court's letter of commendation shortly. Now if we can get an officer to escort the Judge home . . ." They might not believe the story, but they would've been glad for any excuse not to arrest you. Busting someone like you just makes their job that much harder. I don't mean to upset you any more than you are already, but you know it's bad, very bad, for morale all across the law-enforcement community.

So it was just your average, garden-variety bust, as average as the bust of a blind man's place can be, anyway. Blind Chuck probably heard the cops sneak up and deploy as only a blind man can hear, and told everybody to shut up so he could listen, but his old lady said it was nothing, party on. And then there they were, the cops, shining lights in everybody's eyes and throwing them on the floor, even Chuck, whose blank eyes don't spook them anymore. Then hauling everybody to their feet and shining their lights in their eyes again to see how stoned they are until they get to you, Your Honor. Then it's shit or go blind time for the chota. If only I'd been there with my gift of gab to get you out of that scene.

Well, Judge, here they come again. Booking time. They might bond you or they might let you out OR, who knows, but take my advice, tell the media out there no comment for now, that you'll have a statement for them soon. And when you do, make sure you go for the sympathy. The same sympathy you were finally getting for us—make them feel that for you. Make them walk a mile in your shoes—or should I say, make them ride a mile on your bus. You'll beat this rap, Judge. You heard it from me, Theodore Lee James III. You are not a congenital loser. One fucked-up period does not a congenital loser make. It only makes you stronger. Wiser. So chin up, Your Honor. Go forth, beat this thing, and we'll see you down the line.

Vigil

A DISTANT COMMOTION commingles with the cacophony of *Cops*. A slamming of car doors, a man's bark, a woman's fuck yous: all these things happening on Officer O'Riley's televised Pittsburgh beat are finding an echo outside ex-deputy Tony Vigil's Santa Fe home.

The thirty-five-year-old former sheriff's deputy gets up and peers down Vigil Lane. The window, coated with fine caliche road dust, glows bloodred with the sunset; he can't see much. In any case, the altercation out there seems to have stopped; maybe it was just his imagination, or some trick of the airwaves. Fights didn't happen much here on the streets of what the six o'clock newsman has earlier called, in a report on the city's real-estate boom, "Santa Fe's tony east side."

Tony, like his name. He gets a kick out of that. Now here's Tony Vigil of tony Vigil Lane on the east side looking out his window, doing Neighborhood Watch. A kick como una pata' en los huevos, because these news reports have got him thinking about selling this little house and moving to the west side, or Española, or Albuquerque. That's what you had to do when you lost your job and property taxes were rising. Sell your place to the rich gringada and, ¡vámonos, cabrón! The gabachos paid big bucks to live here. They loved the air, they said, the light. They loved winding dirt roads like this one, Vigil Lane, named for his family. They loved to build their mansions out of adobes made from the native soil. The only thing that worried them, according to the newsman, was the growing resentment of the natives, as those natives found themselves displaced from their old barrios. The city's tourism department had recently been forced to pull its ad campaign, "Mi casa es su casa," because it was all too true. It hit too close to home.

Ex-deputy Vigil cracks another Schlitz and wipes the dusty television screen with his sleeve. He wears this blue sweat shirt and matching blue athletic pants day and night now. His wife, who shortly after his dismissal from the sheriff's office had begun attending some kind of support group to learn how to handle their new situation, called them his pajamas. "Let me know when you're out of your pajamas and are dealing with the real world, Tony, and I'll be back," she said before going to stay with her sister in Albuquerque. That's the kind of talk she learned from the group. Tough love.

Officer O'Riley on TV is now wrestling with the perp, a scrawny, tattooed white subject with rivulets of blood running down either side of his face like fake sideburns. And now his wife, who earlier had smashed the bottle over her skinny husband's head, is screaming at the cops not to hurt him. The officers haul him to his feet and Mirandize him. He whines, with an expression like a beaten dog, "Why're you doin' this to me, honey?" Now she's wringing her hands; sure as shooting she'll decline to press charges, and then she'll retract her statement to the police and refuse to cooperate with the prosecutors. It was always this way with domestics; the ex-deputy had seen it a hundred times. The best thing to do, in his experience, is pop them both for disturbing the peace. Instead, the police on camera here politely ask the man if the cuffs are too tight. So much for reality TV.

This was reality: a year ago, a call had crackled in over the deputy's police radio about a domestic on the far west side, off Agua Fría road. It was an address he knew well. It was a scene he knew well. The individual called Locoyote by the people of the barrio was standing in the dust in front of his girlfriend's house, yelling. The records listed Locoyote as Hispanic, but he was half-Anglo—Coyote—with very light-brown, almost yellow, eyes. And he was certifiably loco—the records did reflect that. That night he was naked but covered with dust and dirt, like a Hopi mud person. He held a kitchen knife at his side; it flashed under the bare bulb of the porch light. He crouched and twirled in a bizarre dance, the blade spinning invisible threads around him. But he knew his cocoon wouldn't protect him from Deputy Vigil's gun, because he kept yelling, "Shoot me, bro. For God and country and this puta over here, blow me away." He writhed and shook. Then came his lunge at the officers, the disputed lunge. The girlfriend, who was watching from the steps, and who had been the one to call 911, would later testify that there had been no lunge.

And this was reality: demonstrations were called by a militant new Chicano group called La Raza Renacida to protest the shooting of a brother by the lackey Tío Taco cops of the Anglo rich. The police-review board and the grand jury cleared the deputy, but La Raza forced the formation of a citizens' round table on police-community relations. For several hours every week the sheriff's department and the deputy had to endure unending insults and ridicule from a parade of Chicano-power cholos. The cholos said the chotas were cowards, shooting a naked man armed only with a knife. They ridiculed the deputy's rash statement that he had shot the man for his—the man's—"own protection." They said the chotas were committing genocide against the Hispanic people for the sake of the Anglo newcomer. They said Deputy Vigil was the essence of this cowardly, sellout hispano—hey, this pig even lives on the Anglo east side, among his masters.

A few months later the deputy was fired "for reasons relating to job performance and professional judgment."

"It's just politics," one brother deputy assured him.

"Everything's politics," added another.

"So it's just everything," Deputy Vigil said bitterly.

Now the disturbance has started up again outside the ex-deputy's window. A vehicle comes into view, a chopped-down Chevy Luv with gold hubs and a candy paint job. A young blonde female, about five foot seven and 120 pounds, gets out, slams the passenger door, and strides down the Lane on long Anglo legs. The driver wears a wifebeater and shades and a black-and-red pirate scarf over his head: a cholo punk. This individual creeps alongside the female, saying something out the window at her. She keeps walking, ignoring him. He roars his engine and spins his tires, sending up a plume of dust. Soon they are out of sight.

The ex-deputy jerks open his bureau drawer and unrolls his snub-nosed .38 from a towel. This is his backup piece, the one he used to wear on a shoulder strap. He slips it into the waistband of his pocketless sweat pants, but the elastic doesn't hold the gun and it drops into his crotch; the touch of the cold metal makes him gasp. Not having time to look for his strap, he snatches a Windbreaker from the closet and shoves the revolver into its shallow pocket.

The couple is up ahead, around a bend in the road. The male has gotten out of the vehicle and has the female from behind in a kind of bear hug. His mouth is at her neck, and they are gently swaying. Does he have a weapon against her, is he threatening her? The ex-deputy breaks into a trot. By the time he gets to the scene the female has gotten into her side of the truck and the male is getting into his. The inside of the cab is upholstered in blue crushed velvet with coffin pleats and red piping. The ex-deputy can see no weapon, but he has his own hand tight around the .38 in his front pocket.

"What's happening, bro?"

The cholo looks at the ex-deputy's pocket and a rigidness descends on his face. "Not too much, man." He stares out the windshield and keeps his hands on the chain steering wheel.

The Anglo female, who is very young, speaks: "Hey, there's no problem."

"There never is, miss."

He speaks to the cholo again: "What do you claim, homie?"

"I don't claim nothing, man."

"Where's your barrio, homes? What are you doing over on this side?"

"It's a free country, isn't it?" says the girl. "Leave us alone."

"Where you from, ma'am?"

"What do you mean, where'm I from?" she says indignantly. "I'm a student at St. John's College. Who are—"

The cholo boyfriend doesn't wait for an answer. He throws the Chevy into gear and hauls out.

The air had had this same smell right after the shooting: very pure, but poisonously so, like ozone. Placed on administrative leave, the deputy had stayed home, breathing this air and seeing everything as if at a distance. A state of dissociation, the psychiatrist said. Then, as the investigation dragged on and the demonstrations continued and the citizens' round table started to convene, the air had become close and stale and strangling. The deputy was assigned a desk job.

His brother deputies tried to comfort him by making light of it all.

"What was it that loco was dancing? La última cumbia?"

"'Ya con ésta me despido-o . . .'"

"Well, everyone has their derecho al pataleo, ¿que no?"

Then came the firing. Sheriff Martínez called him into his office for a talk. Sheriff Martínez was a big, burly man who liked to pontificate in twists and turns, through allusions to other things. That morning, the sheriff asked Deputy Vigil if he'd seen the movie Treasure of the Sierra Madre, *with Humphrey Bogart.*

"You know, the one where the mexicanote who says he's a cop is challenged by the gringos to show ID, and he goes, 'Badges? Badges? I don't got to show you no stinkin' badges!' The gringos were on his turf, see."

Deputy Vigil murmured that yes, he'd heard the line.

"Well, sir," said the sheriff, "I'm a mexicano, and you're a

142

mexicano. We've been here how long, the Vigils and the Martínezes? A long time. If this is anybody's turf, it's ours, ¿que no? But when I ask you to turn in your badge, the raza's gonna say, 'Hey, the powers-that-be, the gringos and the big money people, they made Sheriff Martínez fire Deputy Vigil to satisfy the activists, to put a damper on things.' They'll charge scapegoat. But I'm saying that's bullshit, right? I'm a Martínez, saying to a Vigil: that's bullshit, bro . . ."

Deputy Vigil did not force his sheriff to keep trying to explain himself; he placed his badge and his service revolver on his superior's desk, just like in all the TV movies about fired cops.

The ex-deputy, adrenaline pumping, his lungs large, his legs tingling, walks back to his metal-roofed, orange-stuccoed home. It looks tiny next to the many-layered, balconied house going up behind it, a place of double-wide adobes and ponderosa beams, owned by some gringos from California he has never seen. His house looks like a doghouse next to that big one, and right now he does not feel small enough to crawl back inside.

So the ex-deputy walks past his house and continues up Vigil Lane. Venus is punched into the gunmetal sky over the Sangre de Cristos, and the sunset is a bloody bandage over the Navajo Nation, unclotted with cloud. The moon is out too, a brilliant half-moon hinting at some resplendent and inaccessible universe beyond this world: he remembers staring feverishly at the bright moon cut into the outhouse door of his childhood home on Vigil Lane, a child sick on a sunny day, shitting out a batch of bad beans.

At the top of the road is a gated community: Los Miradores. A safe place for the gringada to watch the sunsets and breathe the air, encircled by a massive wrought-iron gate. Behind the gate is a little guardhouse the size of the outhouse, with a twenty-four-hour guard. The ex-deputy's wife, after his firing, had suggested he apply for a security job there. They'd grab you up, she said. You're a trained professional. She was probably right. They'd like an ex-cop who'd shot a cholo perp. Put the fear into the marauding cholada just knowing he was there.

Right below Los Miradores is the college, St. John's, the school the girl with the cholo said she went to. Maybe the ex-deputy could apply for a security job there, too. What would be his main duty? Arresting boys for date rape? That was the big crime on college campuses these days. That's all you heard about anymore on Geraldo or Oprah. That girl . . . soon enough she would be coming to him, crying date rape. Güerita pendeja. What would he tell her? That she got what she had coming, no?

As he heads down Camino de la Cruz Blanca, he hears a faint crunching coming from behind the tennis courts: someone running on the college track. The track is red pumice, but in the failing light it looks black as asphalt. The crunching gets louder as the individual rounds the corner toward him. The individual is a female. His scrotum tightens. Last year there had been a widely reported rape here: a Hispanic subject had dragged a student off the running track and into the arroyo.

Obscured behind a poplar, he watches her round the track another time, and then another. Her stride is smooth, self-confident; her proud blonde head glows in the moonlight. The third time she comes around, he emerges from the shadows.

"Ma'am you shouldn't—"

She stops midstride, her foot coming down hard on the pumice. She stumbles backward but doesn't quite fall. She points something at him, some kind of key chain.

"Ma'am, I'm a police officer. It's getting dark. You shouldn't—"

She backs away, still pointing the business end of the key chain at him. He realizes she has no reason to believe him; he's not in uniform. The words of his dismissal report—"lack of professional judgment"—come back to him. But he's angry now, and he keeps advancing toward her, his voice louder. "Ma'am, I'm telling you, you shouldn't be here. For your own protection, you shouldn't be in this area at all—"

She sprints through the rabbitbrush toward her vehicle. For a moment he feels like leaping after her, grabbing her, slapping some hard sense into her. She reaches her car; keys jangle frantically in the lock. She jumps in and tears off.

He feels the adrenaline again, smells the ozone clearness. He knows he should ditch the .38 now, but he doesn't. Back on Camino Cabra, on his way home, he can hear it behind him, the tiger purr of one of the new city cruisers. He keeps walking, down the road, down into his ancestral claim. In another minute the spot will stab him in the back. They will spread-eagle him against the cruiser and search him, they will find the gun, they will demand that he identify himself, but he will have nothing, no badge or ID to prove he is their brother, Deputy Tony Vigil of the Santa Fe Sheriff's Department. When they cuff him, he will not bow his head, and will keep his eyes on the cold stars.

Backing Up

CHILL AIR STRUCK Danny Sánchez when he entered his home that Christmas night, and it made him shiver, but he didn't think anything was wrong at first. It was just that adobe wasn't a good insulator, despite people's romantic view of it as such. Tourists gazed out from their cars at places like his and thought, *What cozy little huts those are, huddled in the snow, windows glowing warmly in their thick sills, rounded stucco walls like soft brown blankets.* But Danny knew better because his father was a building contractor and had always bitched about adobe. Earlier that day, over Christmas turkey at his parents' place, his father had complained about a house he was building in the east mountains for some California gringos, about how they insisted it be a Pueblo-revival adobe even though it made no sense to build a flat-roofed adobe in a place that got that much snow. "Ah, qué gringos," his father said, "just because they're in New Mexico they think they must conform to the Santa Fe look." Danny, glancing around at the glutinous holiday feast—the gravy, the yams, the stuffing—was about to say, *Well, look at how we're conforming to this gringo food; we never eat this kind of thing except on Christmas and Thanksgiving.* But he didn't, of course, because he didn't want to hurt his mother's feelings or make his father mad. His mother made the best posole and menudo and salsa de chile pequín he'd ever tasted, but on these two holidays it was never anything but this bland American food, which no one in the family, he believed, really liked.

Now Danny was back in the small adobe casita he rented in Albuquerque's San Ysidro barrio. He might have stayed the night at his parents' place in the Heights, but a powdery snow had begun to fall up there and he didn't want to get snow-bound. He had his master's thesis to work on here at home, and the Christmas break was a good time to make headway on it.

He paused in the tiny zaguán, his head almost grazing the age-blackened vigas, and breathed in the coolness. This narrow vestibule flanked by a scalloped wall reminded him of the key-hole entrances to the ancient Anasazi dwellings at Chaco. Archaeologists speculated that they were so designed to force intruders to place their hands on the walls and enter head first, thus exposing their throats to the flint of the occupants.

Danny flattened his hands against the walls and thrust his head forward into the chill air, in imitation of such an intruder. The walls felt downright icy, and a strange, cold breeze brushed across his face.

Alarmed now, he strode through the living room and straight into the low room in the back he used as his study. The gauze curtain of the north window billowed in the breeze as in a thousand horror movies. He glanced at the computer hutch and wondered, for a stunned moment, why he was admiring its curved, many-shelved functionality. Then he realized he was seeing it without its clutter of computer and monitor and modem and printer. Those things were gone.

He knew that this was a moment he'd remember vividly for the rest of his life, standing there in the cold, staring at the place where his computer had been. And he knew, in a circular implosion of awareness, that he knew it was such a moment. *I will always remember standing here, knowing I will always remember standing here, knowing I will always remember standing here. . . . Realizing my computer was gone with its hard drive and a year and a half of work. My thesis. Which I hadn't bothered to back up.*

His gaze shot to the table where his tape recorder normally stayed, and he saw that it was gone too. And so was the little wooden box in which he kept his recordings of all those interviews with the homeboys, the gangbangers, and the torcidos that formed the original material for that thesis.

His tongue went thick and dry. He stepped carefully into the kitchen and took a glass from the cabinet, deliberately, remembering his every move and remembering he was remembering, as if he now had to record everything in the computer of his mind. He filled the glass and drank, and it disappeared in him like water in a dry arroyo and he was still thirsty. He drank again, but it did no good.

They hadn't taken the telephone. He called 911. The operator asked him where he was calling from, and when he told her San Ysidro, she inquired, wearily now, whether he wanted to file the report over the phone or if he wanted an officer to actually go to the scene.

"You mean you don't always investigate?" Danny asked, his voice a croak.

"I can send an officer to the scene, sir, but it won't be immediately."

A gust of wind whistled through the broken pane. Shards of glass glinted on the floor. He shuddered.

"I'll wait. But if I close the window they came through, I'll disturb the evidence, won't I?"

"That's up to you, sir."

It was snowing harder now, a swirling, crazy snow, flakes flying back up to the orange-lit clouds. He shuddered again. He wanted a real drink now, a shot of liquor, but he only had a cold beer in the refrigerator, too cold. He stared at the empty salt-shaker on the dinette table. A house without salt, his mother always said, was hexed.

He called home. His mother answered.

"Ay, hijo," she said when he told her what had happened.

She was good with the ay, hijos. Even when good things happened it was ay, hijo. When he told her he was going to pursue the master's degree, it had been ay, hijo. It was no good explaining to her what it meant to have lost the information he had lost, because she didn't understand what he was working on or what this information was for. Even loss of material goods meant little to her, because she had grown up with nothing. Only death of a loved one seemed significant to her.

"I want to die, Ma," Danny said.

"¡Qué cosas dices, Danny! I'm going to send your Papi to get you."

"No, Ma. No. It's okay. It's under control. The cops are coming."

His father took the phone.

"They got everything, que no, hijo," he said in his annoyed, I-told-you-so voice.

His father had never approved of Danny's moving to San Ysidro. Sure, he was proud Daniel was working on a master's, but it was one thing to study what had gone wrong in the barrio—why it had gone from a relatively peaceful semi-rural enclave of tinsmiths and garlic growers to a nesting ground for some of Albuquerque's worst street gangs—and another to choose to live there, to actually move to this sagging adobe in the midst of the misery. They'd had a serious argument about it, in fact, with his father, who had grown up in San Ysidro but who now lived in the mostly white Heights, shouting something about his son wanting to "waller in poverty." "Why waller in it?" he said, using this word, *waller*, a gringo word he'd picked up from a Texan client. "You can't walk away from your roots," Danny shot back, and for a minute he thought his father might hit him. "You know what was the smartest saying to come out of the Chicano movimiento you admire so much?" his father said, his anger quaking. "Sal si puedes. Get out if you can."

"Well, they took everything that counts, Dad," Danny said now. "My thesis. Son of a bitch, they stole my thesis!"

"They stole your thesis? Who'd want to steal your thesis?"

"They stole the computer, Dad. All my stuff was on the hard drive, and I hadn't backed to floppies."

"You hadn't what?"

"Backed up. God, you stupid, fucking dumbshit!" He felt like weeping. "Not you, Dad. Me."

"¡Calma, hijo! Listen, if I can get out of the driveway, I'm coming over."

"No, Dad, don't come. Please. The streets are terrible. The cops are here. I gotta go. I'll call you back."

It was a lone cop, a big, buzz-cut white guy with buffed, tattooed arms. Officer Kronski. He belonged to the Gang Unit, thanks to complaints by the citizens' group Barrios United, who said an all-Hispanic Gang Unit implied that gangs were only a Hispanic phenomenon. So the chief threw in this white token. Danny supposed he could relate well enough to the skinheads, but here in the barrio he was worse than useless if relating to the raza was part of the job. Pinche chota cabeza de zacate seco was how Danny referred to him in interviews with gangbangers, to break the ice and get a laugh out of them, because his flattop was a miniature field of winter grass.

"Officer Kronski," Danny said. "How's it going?"

Officer Kronski's brow wrinkled in meaty perplexity, trying to place him.

"Oh, yeah, the guy who studies gangs. Well, then, you probably know more about who did this than I do. Who'd you let in?"

"Nobody."

And that was true, if what the cop meant was gangbangers. He'd never invited any of those homies into his home. To do so would be to let them lay claim to it, and that would invite hostility from rival gangs. No, he had to keep his place neutral; he knew that.

But now he'd invited in this other gangbanger, the cop, a member of what the cops liked to call the city's biggest, baddest gang—the Albuquerque Police Department. And that had been a mistake, he now realized. Gangbangers knew where he lived, and they would notice the squad car parked out there in front and wonder what was up with the cops. They'd think he was punking it. Now he wished the chota would just go away. The cop was taking his time, though, snooping around the house, as if Danny were the bad guy. What was he looking for? Dope? Or did he suspect Danny was making a false police report to collect on insurance or something?

"I'm not insured," Danny said. "And anyway, the stuff wasn't worth anything. An old 386 computer. The tapes of my interviews. It's the information on it that's valuable."

"Okay, we'll put that in the report. Let me go out to the car for the forms."

"No," said Danny. "It's no use. They'd erase the information on the hard drive. And even if they didn't, I didn't park the heads, so it's gotten all messed up anyway. I've got no data left."

"So you don't want to make a report."

"No. Forget it."

The cop looked at him hard, nibbling his gum between his front teeth.

"You know, they blame cops for blaming the victim," he said. "But sometimes I really think people ask for it. What did you think was going to happen to your stuff, living down here? Next time you don't want our help, don't call. Merry Christmas."

Danny wiped moisture from the front window and watched the cop drive away. Fuck you too. He peered down the street, wondering if anyone had seen the chota enter or leave his house. Homies weren't chilling outside tonight—it was too cold for that. The sureños were no doubt kicking it, as they did every night, at Chango's around the block, and though they kept their collective eye on the street, a scout didn't always go out into the cold to scope out every cop that drove by. So they wouldn't *necessarily* know Danny had punked it tonight by calling the chota.

Danny paced the house, swinging his arms as if warming up for Tae Kwon Do class, taking big gulps of air. He needed to talk with someone, but someone who understood his loss better than his parents did. A colleague, a fellow grad student, someone in his own gang at the university.

He dialed Raúl.

"Bummer," said Raúl. "No backups? No hard copy?"

Was he gloating? There was something of that in his voice. Raúl, it suddenly occurred to Danny, was no compa. He was a competitor. That's what school was, dog-eat-dog, every student grasping for limited space and funds and attention from professors. Now Danny regretted he'd phoned him as much as he regretted having called his parents and the cops. He didn't want anyone at school to know he'd lost his research. He weakened at the prospect of having to face his faculty advisor and his thesis committee. They would write him off as a loser.

"No big deal," he told Raúl, trying to sound casual now. "I can pretty well reconstruct my argument. Hey, listen, man, I gotta go."

Loser. Danny's main informant was a sureño called Loser, the word proudly tattooed in Old English lettering across the back of his neck. With Loser as his inspiration, Danny's thesis came down to the simple idea that street gangs were nothing more than support networks for youths that considered themselves, in the large scope of things, losers, and his task was to show how those networks functioned. The irony of Loser, as a successful gangbanger, was that he had all the makings of a winner in his self-assurance as a loser. Danny often wished he himself had that kind of self-confidence as a scholar—he would need it if he intended to remain in academia, for that was a place that had no room for failures.

Danny wandered into his study and stared at the broken window. A snowflake wafted through the jagged hole and landed on a drop of blood he hadn't noticed before. Fed by the moisture, the droplet swelled and trembled. He touched it, then stared at the redness that collected in the ridges of his finger.

There it was—the guy's, or the girl's, DNA. That droplet kept the record of his or her whole being, if you believed modern science. Everything you needed to know about what drove him or her through that window was encoded in those molecules. It made behavioral research like his a little obsolete. These days, supposedly all you had to do was find the "loser" gene, or genes.

He brought the fingertip to his mouth. He touched the blood to his tongue, tasted the salt. He felt light-headed, giddy, moving toward something new in the vacuum of his loss.

Danny had never been to any gang-house parties, especially late at night. His research didn't require it. He knew what went on there, the doping, the drinking, the ranking in, the working up of courage to do a drive-by, the celebration after a successful action, the mourning for a fallen soldier. Those parties were the soul of gang life, they were where the group bonding took place, where the hot energy collected and achieved critical mass. But the interviews he conducted with Loser and the others in the serenity of a café or the student union gave him a good enough idea of those activities. He didn't need to party with them, even if they'd let him. Still, it felt strange to be at home writing about them, knowing they were right around the corner at Chango's. When once he told his father about his research methods, his father asked him why he had to live in San Ysidro at all, and Danny didn't have an answer for that.

Now he knew why he lived here. He had a claim to it.

He stepped outside. The wind teared his eyes. A swirl of snow and barrio dust deviled down the street. He pictured the snow pristine and soft on his parents' slope-roofed house in the Heights, like the cover of a Christmas card.

Chango's house glowed under the orange city sky. The yellow light inside seemed wholly contained: it didn't seep out the windows or touch the snow. The house was a small gray cube with chicken wire showing in places through the scratch coat, waiting for a stucco job that would never come. It was what Danny's father scornfully called the I-give-up look, and it was common enough in the barrio. Danny thought in Chango's case it was maybe a deliberate look, because it gave the place a bunker-like aspect, like concrete reinforced with steel. Galvanized steel roof gutters jutted from the parapets like bright cannon.

Parked in the dirt yard behind the cracked cinder-block wall sat two Chevy lowriders, one painted in flat black primer, the other candy-apple red. Loser opened the door before Danny knocked. Hip-hop and hot, moist air tumbled out the door and enveloped him. He smelled posole cooking, starchy corn cut by the sharpness of chile and tripe.

"The li'l prof," said Loser. "Sup." Loser had a black knit cap pulled down to his glittery black eyes, and his lips were clownish with red chile. He wore a black funeral T whose ornate white lettering read, "In Loving Memory of My Homie, Frankie Bashful Sánchez."

"Hey," Danny said. He could never bring himself to call him Loser, but it seemed aloof to call him by his real name, Leandro.

Before his glasses steamed up, Danny glimpsed several people around a kitchen table lit warmly by a bare, yellow bulb. One of them—Chango—lazily swept what to Danny looked like a large revolver off the table and onto his lap. Chango was a veterano, maybe thirty, with the sucked-in cheeks of a junkie and an Abe Lincoln beard that gave him an apelike look. He'd never been one of Danny's better informants, because he wasn't much of a talker. If he'd ever been a talker, prison and dope had taken it out of him. The feds had tried to seize the house after his latest bust, but they had to give it back because it belonged to Chango's mother. Danny wondered if the viejita was in some back room, doing whatever moms do when their house is full of gangbangers.

"Close the door and get the vato a beer," a girl with a hoarse voice cried. She was sunk so low in a sofa that it looked like she'd never be able to get up.

"Give him a tequilazo," someone else said. "Dude looks cold."

Someone thrust a large square bottle into his hand. Danny said "salud" and drank a slug. It burned his tongue. He passed the bottle to Loser and wiped his glasses.

"What's your name, bro?" the girl asked. Her bangs arched stiff as claws, and her lipstick had been licked away to a thin purple line at the edges.

"Danny."

"Danny's a pussy placa. A joto name. What's a good name? Angel or Jesús. Why aren't you Angel or Jesús?"

She was fucked up. Loser looked at her almost pityingly.

"If he was down with us, we'd give him a placa," she said.

"But he ain't down," someone said.

"Ain't down for the set? Don't got a claim on the sur? Then what the fuck's he doing here?"

"I got ripped off," Danny said.

Chango tipped back in his chair and turned down the radio behind him. Everyone at the kitchen table looked at Danny.

Danny turned to Loser. "You know all those interviews I did with you? All the stuff for my thesis? It's gone."

"This guy's gonna make us *famous*, man!" said Loser. "Sureños fuckin *rule*, ese."

For a fleeting moment, Danny imagined the thieves discovering his work on the computer and going on to get it published, a curious case of plagiarism—self-plagiarism, in a sense, if the thieves were the very gangbangers he'd interviewed.

"I'm not shitting you, bro. It's gone. I didn't make any backups."

"Don't got no backups? Gotta have backups in the barrio, bro. This my backup Puppet, there's Chango, this is Sad Girl."

Sad Girl, the girl on the sofa, placed her splayed index finger, thumb, and little finger over her heart, her other two fingers folded: love for my homies.

The tequila bottle appeared in Danny's hand again, and as he tilted his head back he glanced around the room. No computer here, from what he could see.

"Got insurance, bro?" Loser asked.

"You can't insure what I lost."

"You can't insure the best things, huh, bro?" someone called from the kitchen.

155

"You can't insure me?" Sad Girl said.

"Hoo, qué loca. The premiums'd be more than the payoff on you, Sad Girl!"

Sad Girl looked pleased.

"We're your insurance, Sad Girl," came the voice from the kitchen.

The liquor was getting to Danny's head. He felt warm inside and out. The vapors of the boiling posole and menudo wafting from the kitchen reminded him of when he was a boy, of the small house they lived in before his parents moved to the many-storied one in the Heights.

"This guy got no insurance," Loser said. "Got no backups."

"Got nothin'," someone said.

"A loser," someone else said.

"Loser too?" said Loser, holding his fingers in a V. "We're tocayos, then. Brothers." His fingers curled around each other.

"No, I liked what you called him," Sad Girl said to Loser.

"Li'l Prof?" Loser pinched the glasses from Danny's face.

"I can't see without those, bro," said Danny.

"So we'll get you a blind guy's dog," Sad Girl said. "A pit bull."

"Can be your road dog," someone else said. "Your backup."

Danny reached for his glasses. A bottle crashed against his forehead and splintered. Cold beer foamed in his ears, his legs wobbled, and he fell to the ground. Feet hammered him from all sides. He got to his knees, but the word Nike flew to his face and sent him sprawling on his back.

He covered his head. *They're jumping me in. They're ranking me into the gang. I've got to fight back. I can't back down. I didn't back up and now I can't back down.*

But he couldn't get up. There were too many of them. All he could do was laugh. Though it hurt his ribs, his jaw, all of him, he laughed. He laughed to think he'd deliberately set himself up to lose his work—to fail—so that exactly this would happen.

He tasted his blood in his mouth, warm and salty and good.

Solidarity

ROBERTO SALAZAR'S ONLY campus interview that year was at Southwestern University, in his hometown of Albuquerque. Considering the poor job market for historians, he was lucky to get even this one flyback. He familiarized himself with the work of the faculty members on the hiring committee and learned as much as he could about the history of the department and of the school as a whole. What he failed to do was notice that one of the associate provosts bore the name Dr. Manuel G. Apodaca—and if he did, he failed to realize this was Manny until he was summoned to Dr. Apodaca's office on the top floor of the SWU administration building.

Manny and Roberto greeted one another with back-pounding abrazos. "Manny—you the man!" Roberto said. In his mind, he said, *Manny—you, the Man?* Because it was incredible that Manny had risen so high. Perhaps it was just as incredible to Manny that Roberto was interviewing for a tenure-track professorship. Roberto and Manny, two Albuquerque militants from the '70s, teenage vatos who back then had worn black berets with silver stars and cochineal-red ponchos and gold Aztec-calendar medallions around their necks, now in suits and ties. Roberto had gotten his suit at a thrift store and was unable to button the coat over his paunch; Manny's looked like it was tailored to fit his small frame. Manny's moustache was neatly clipped, but what was most surprising was that it was completely *white*.

Manny, leaning back in his oxblood executive chair, fingers laced across his chest, asked Roberto how it felt to be back home. Roberto, sitting in a spotlight slice of sunlight, replied that he'd forgotten how bright the New Mexico sun was, even now in February: it warmed like a slug of tequila. Regretting the reference to alcohol, he babbled on about seasonal affective disorder, or SAD, a syndrome that affected a lot of people in the gray-skied Midwest where he now lived—though it had never bothered him, he lied.

Manny, white moustache spreading in a smile, reminded him that this was not an interview; associate provosts were not normally involved in faculty hiring. And tonight, Manny said, Roberto was invited to something equally unofficial—a barbacoa at the old place, in the South Valley.

"Your grandfather's place? The ranchito? I can't believe it."

"Like old times," Manny said. He gazed steadily at Roberto for a moment, then produced a book from his desk drawer. It was Roberto's book, the book that made him a contender for this tenure-track job: *Chotas and Chicanos: Police Repression of the Chicano Movimiento*. Roberto signed it for him "con solidaridad"—with solidarity—his hand trembling enough to make the letters wavy as a child's.

Following a late-afternoon interview with the department chair and a tour of the campus by one of the search-committee members, Roberto returned to his hotel. He'd rented a car at his own expense, thereby proving his self-sufficiency as well as his familiarity with Albuquerque, not to mention saving busy faculty from having to shuttle him around—all of which would score him a few points with the committee, he hoped.

As he showered and changed into casual clothes, he thought about the grandfather's ranchito in the South Valley. Amazing that the abuelo was still alive. Well, the viejitos lived a long time in the Valley. Did he still have those fighting cocks, each tethered to a post in front of its little house? Was the shed still there—the one he and Manny and the others had built the pipe bombs in?

And how much did Manny know about Roberto's quick breakdown and confession during his interrogation by the cops, after the bust for the bombs? Roberto's father decided to move the family out of state—did Manny know this move was, at least in part, to get Roberto out of reach of reprisal from his radical accomplices, including Manny, should they discover his treachery?

Roberto eyed the minibar beneath the television, but he had to be careful: the hotel bill would be processed by the university, and it was better that it not show that he'd consumed alcohol. Better to buy something at a convenience store on his way to the barbecue—one or two of those miniature bottles of liquor he remembered they sold in New Mexico.

He floated—these rental cars were so luxurious—to a 7-Eleven some blocks south of the hotel. The air was chilly now that the sun had set—not ideal barbecue weather, but Albuquerque people liked to believe they lived in the warm desert. The miniatures were kept in locked plexiglass cabinets behind the counter. He asked for two José Cuervos—make it three, what the hell—and some breath mints.

As the skinny clerk was inserting the miniatures into tiny paper sacks, he looked past Roberto and piped in a lilting East Indian voice, "You must pay for the merchandise, sir!"

The hooded cholo to whom the clerk had spoken answered by jamming a fist deep in the pocket of his baggy pants, as though reaching for a gun or knife. In his other hand he lugged a case of Tecate. He shouldered open the door of the store and strode out with the beer.

The clerk was on the phone with the police instantly: "He is in the parking lot."

At the edge of the lot, one foot in the alley, the cholo picked at a corner of the box.

"Possibly armed," said the clerk into the phone. "No. I do not presently see a weapon."

159

The cholo succeeded in extracting a beer from the case. He cracked it open, tilted his head, glugged. He lowered the can, belched—Roberto heard the belch, faintly—and stared defiantly at the store. He was probably only a teenager, but his shaved head and the worry-puckers on his brow and his baggy old man's pants made him seem older. Some tattooed word, most likely his gang placa or nickname, curved around his throat.

The clerk locked the front doors. "I'm sorry about this, sir," he said to Roberto. "But for your own protection, please remain within the premises until the police arrive."

Roberto wondered why the cholo didn't take off. Was he trying to prove some kind of macho point? Maybe this was some kind of gang rite of initiation, some hazing thing?

"Open the doors," Roberto told the clerk.

"I cannot recommend, sir—"

"Let me out," said Roberto.

The clerk cracked the doors just wide enough to let Roberto out and snapped the lock behind him. The cholo moved his hand into his pocket again and stared at Roberto with a look they called . . . what was it? Mad-dogging.

Roberto backed up a step. "Bro," he said. "Carnalito. You need some feria to pay for that?" He made a move for his wallet but thought better of it: better keep his own hands within sight.

The cholo crushed the can in his fist and threw it at Roberto. "I don't need no fuckin' money, ese puto."

The can clattered at Roberto's feet. One time, back in Indiana, a student had wadded up an exam he'd done poorly on and thrown it at Roberto, at the time a graduate teaching assistant, before storming out of the classroom. Roberto liked to think of that student as an overprivileged gringuito with a sense of entitlement who was outraged at being flunked by a Mexican. Now Roberto saw himself through the cholo's glassy eyes: "cool" older guy who thinks he can relate to young people and never tires of telling them he knows where they're at because he's been there too, bro, but that it's really not worth it.

Though why wasn't it worth it, if he was now a cool guy with all kinds of advice based on exciting lived experience?

The cops arrived in three squad cars, one roaring down the alley and two tearing into the parking lot, boxing the cholo in expertly. The cholo grabbed the box of beer and tried to leap over one of the police cars, but his foot slipped on the hood and he fell hard to the ground, the box bursting open beside him. The cops—one of them hispano, the other two white—pounced on him, ground their knees into his back.

"Hey," said Roberto.

They jerked the kid to his feet. He shouted something Roberto heard as "Wuss-I!" He yelled it again, rooster-chested: "Wuss-I!"

The police threw him onto the hood of the squad car. They kicked his feet apart and ran their hands up and down his legs, one of them mechanically reciting his Miranda rights.

The cholo arched his back. "Wuss-I!"

The hispano cop slammed his face into the hood.

"Hey!" said Roberto.

The cop lifted his hand from the cholo's head and turned to Roberto. "You okay, sir?"

"You don't have to, you know—"

"You okay?" the policeman repeated, louder, drawing himself to his full height.

The other two cops pulled their handcuffed suspect off the car. "West Side, huh?" said one. "Well, that's where you're going, homes. Drinking Tecate without a lime, that's a fuckin' felony."

In the struggle, the kid's baggy pants had fallen to his knees, below his boxer shorts. The cops hobbled him to the rear of the patrol car and mashed him behind the cage.

The hispano policeman picked up one of the loose cans of beer and tossed it into the broken box.

"Okay, get going," he told Roberto, without looking at him.

"I'm a witness," said Roberto, his voice quaking. "Don't you have to—"

"Get going, sir."

Roberto's legs shook so badly that on his way out of the lot he ran up over a curb and nearly hit a light pole. The cops watched him with smirks as he backed up and finally succeeded in making his way into the street. He stopped in a strip-mall parking lot and cracked open a miniature with unsteady fingers, dribbling tequila on his leather jacket. These fucking little bottles. A moment later, warmth bloomed from his middle and he felt stronger. Fucking pigs, man. Of course they didn't want to take his statement—he'd testify more to their brutality than to the cholo's theft. He should go back and get their badge numbers. Report them. Though a lot of good that would do. Hadn't he written the book on cops? They always closed ranks.

He finished off the second miniature. Wuss-I? That's what he'd heard the cholo say. West Side. Name of his barrio, presumably. The turf he "represented." Shout it out, bro. In Roberto's day, that cholo would've been a Brown Beret or a Crusader for Justice or a La Raza militant. But, as his book attested, the cops—the State Police, the FBI, the local sheriff's departments—had, through infiltration and dirty tricks and outright murder, decimated the Movimiento's ranks; or, in the words of one FBI agent, "reduced them to banditry." Or if they got lucky, they became academics like himself or administrators like Manny.

He got to Manny's abuelo's place on automatic pilot, remembering the way even after all these years. He turned onto the cottonwood-lined lane, and the caliche dust thrown up by the car in front of him, dust mixed with the scent of dope, flung him back in memory into the shed where Manny's abuelo kept the rooster feed, and where Roberto and Manny would pass crackling jubies of seedy weed back and forth and watch the cars go by on the road and talk about the coming Revolution and the new Chicano nation of Aztlán, and into what lengths they should hacksaw the pipe, the first step in making the bombs.

The old place looked much the same: long front portal with a sagging roof, ground under the elms grassless and dusty, and, yes, the fighting cocks, roosting for the night on top of their houses, heads under their wings, each with his foot chained to

162

its post, the houses like identical little dog houses, painted white. Amazing to Roberto was not that the abuelo still raised them—New Mexico allowed you to breed gamecocks, though it was illegal to actually fight them—but that Manny was bold enough to invite university faculty here and risk being criticized by animal-rights people. That said something about his power and job security, Roberto supposed. Or about his ability to smooth ruffled feathers—which he'd always been good at, literally and figuratively. As a teenager, Roberto had watched him scoop up furious roosters and hold them in the crook of his arm and stroke their heads until their elastic eyelids hooded their fierce eyes. The one time Roberto had tried this, the rooster sunk its battle-hardened talons into his belly and jabbed its beak into the ball of his thumb. With a shriek, he thrust the animal away, and it bounced off the ground and came back at him, attacking his legs as he fled to the safety of the shed and his guffawing clica.

Manny had assured Roberto that the gathering tonight was "unofficial," but Roberto knew that no encounter with faculty or staff could be guaranteed off the record for a job candidate on a campus visit. Two of the search committee members were on the porch: Helen and Troy, Helen dowdy and sweet, Troy somewhat black and somewhat brash. They made much silly fun of their name combination and formed a good-cop-bad-cop team, Helen at the committee interview lobbing him softballs about his teaching methods, Troy bearing down on Roberto's reasons for wanting to leave his current position at the community college in Indiana (as if that wasn't obvious—it was a community college in Indiana, and he was a lowly adjunct). His recent divorce, another incentive to want to start a new life, was nobody's business.

Helen sipped red wine and Troy had a Bud and Manny, now in jeans, beat-up loafers, and a barbecuer's stained apron, kept a Corona on the leaf of his grill. It seemed to Roberto that if he didn't partake, he'd seem uptight. Uncollegial, even. Besides, he still felt shaky from the run-in with the police. He plunged his hand in the icy cooler and fished out a Tecate. Salud, carnalito.

"I got a chance to finish your book this afternoon," Helen told him. "Wonderful research."

"Well, I see the police haven't gotten much better around here," Roberto said. And he told them about the incident he'd just witnessed at the 7-Eleven.

"What was unusual, in my experience with these things," said Roberto, "was how after the carnalito yelled 'West Side,' the police said that's where they were going to take him. Now, I know about cops dumping a gangbanger off in enemy turf—real nice, right?—but to take him back to his own? Obviously they figured that after roughing him up like that, they'd just drop him off in front of his homies so they could all see the direct consequences of messing with the Man."

"Oh, no, no, no, no, no," said Troy, a patronizing little laugh tripping through the nos. "What they mean is that they're going to take him to the West Side jail."

"Ah."

"Way out on the mesa," Troy continued. "On the way there, that's when they really beat the shit out of them."

"I see."

"Professor Salazar," Manny said, coming up behind him and taking him by the elbow. "There's someone out back you're going to want to say hi to."

The abuelo was burning trash in the same cinder-block incinerator into whose fire Roberto, Manny, and two other vatos had thrown an unopened can of Pepsi, waiting an eternity for it to explode and send ashes and embers and bits of unburned trash all over the place. The roosters had gone crazy, leaping into the air and beating their wings, and the boys had run around stomping the embers out. The abuelo, fortunately, was not at home, and afterward the boys had made jokes about the cops, the fucking chotas, blowing sky-high like those ashes, though they knew there would be no chotas inside the cars they intended to bomb. Not that anybody was against offing a pig, they assured one another, but the only way to do the "action" without getting caught was to put the pipe bombs under empty chotamobiles at night.

"Abuelo, Roberto Salazar is here," Manny said. "You remember the Salazars?"

"Know a lot of Salazars," said the abuelo, poking at the fire.

"These were the ones that left."

"Ah, ésos."

"Well, we're back now," Roberto said helplessly. "I am, I mean."

The abuelo turned and gazed at him, the reflected flames flickering in his filmy eyes. "I remember you," he said.

Behind the abuelo stood the shed, the shed where they'd begun to build the pipe bombs. The light from the fire played on the table vice, the same one, Roberto supposed, that had held the pipes he and Manny and the others sawed and drilled, as well the thin sheets of steel that the abuelo cut to make spurs for the gamecocks.

The advantage of canned beer like Tecate, as opposed to those clear-bottled Coronas, was that nobody could tell by looking when you were low, and if you were quick you could snag a new one without anyone noticing and people would think you were still nursing your old one.

At some point Manny offered him a wedge of lime to go with his beer, which gave Roberto the opportunity to act as though he'd forgotten he even had a beer.

"Ah, here it is. Thank you, carnal. As that cop said to the carnalito at the 7-Eleven, Tecate without a lime is a fuckin' felony. Or should be."

A couple of people hadn't heard the whole story, so he told it again. This time he mentioned his misinterpretation of the cholo's cry.

"You thought he was saying *what*?"

"I don't know, like, 'Wuss I, wuss I!'? Something like that." Now Roberto regretted bringing up that part.

"That's pretty funny," someone said. "Not exactly wussy, standing up to the cops."

"That's right!" Roberto said. "He stood up to the fucking chotas."

Manny steered Roberto away from the group and toward the barbecue. "Here, let's get you something to eat."

He watched Roberto spear the brisket. "I'm looking forward to reading your book."

"The pen is mightier than the sword, ¿que no?"

The next day being a workday, people soon began to leave. Roberto gave Manny a good-bye abrazo and a brown-power handshake.

"You're okay, right?" said Manny, looking him in the face.

"Hombre, of course."

Manny wished him luck with the job.

Roberto went around the porch to say good-bye to the abuelo. No abuelo. The fire was ember low and the shed dark. He wondered what the abuelo meant by that "I remember you." In what way did he remember him? As the kid who had punked out his grandson, sung like a sinsonte as soon as he'd gotten busted, which had led to the police raid on the ranchito? But how could the abuelo, how could anyone, be sure of what had truly transpired way back then? Again, the chotas had used so many tricks—disinformation, poison-pen letters, planted evidence—to destroy the Movimiento. His book told all about it.

He trudged down the caliche driveway to his rental car. He was okay: tired, yes, but not unsteady. And even if he was a little buzzed, what he beheld sobered him like a pail of ice water: a State Police car, driving slowly into the ranchito. Roberto watched as the unit parked next to his rental. The cop got out, and Roberto approached.

"There a problem, officer?"

The policeman, a young hispano, slender in his black uniform, regarded him quizzically. The radio crackled behind him.

Roberto reared back. "A Chicano state chota! What a shame. Qué pena, raza."

The policeman glanced at the house, then back at Roberto.

"It's okay, officer. Everything's under control. Just a get-together with the provost of the university. No gangs here. No revolutionaries, either."

Finally the cop spoke. "How much have you had to drink tonight, sir?"

Ah, the old question. Órale pues. "I don't really have to answer that, ¿que no? Unless I'm driving. Shit, even if I am driving. But let's play the game. Two beers. That's what they all say, right? Two."

"Two forty-ounce?"

The kid had already learned his pig sarcasm.

"You worried about it, officer? Give me the test. Give me the pinche eye test. Go ahead."

The test was called the horizontal gaze nystagmus test. Roberto knew all about it. It was inadmissible in most jurisdictions, but the cops, in their arrogance, continued to use it. If you failed it, they made you do the Breathalyzer or drew your blood.

The young cop took a pen from his shirt pocket, then told Roberto to follow its tip with his eyes as he slowly swept it back and forth. Roberto knew what he was looking for: a rapid trembling of the eyeballs when they got to the edge of their sockets. This happened to intoxicated people; but it also happened to people with neurological problems of various sorts, and sometimes to those who were merely tired or nervous, which was why the courts had struck it down.

"Look at the pen, not at me," said the policeman.

Roberto kept his eyes locked on the treasonous young Chicano's for another moment before acquiescing to follow the pen's slow movement. As his eyes turned to the left, they caught sight of Manny coming down the porch steps.

"Everything okay out here?" he called.

Roberto and the policeman stared at each other and didn't answer.

Manny broke into a little trot. "Dr. Salazar," he said. "Dr. Salazar, I'd like you to meet my son, Rudolfo." And to the policeman: "Rudy, this is Professor Roberto Salazar."

Oh, Manny. Carnal. Why didn't you tell me before? You'll say, *Why didn't you ask, the way one always asks about family, if one has any educación at all?* But it's not like that, and you know it. We have to avoid the personal. I don't ask you, and so you don't feel obliged to ask me. Because that might be illegal, ¿que no? EEOC rules, and all that. I am, after all, interviewing for a job.

But what else to do now but offer Manny's son his hand? The policeman hesitated, but took it, briefly, before turning to his father. "Can't stay but a minute, Dad, but I happened to be in the neighborhood. Abuelo still up?"

"You bet," said Manny. And to Roberto, "Come on back to the house with us, Professor. Stay a little longer."

"I should go," Roberto murmured. "Got to get up early."

"Interview with the dean at eight thirty tomorrow, right?"

"Yes." How did Manny know that? And why? He wasn't involved in faculty hiring, he'd said.

Roberto turned to Officer Martínez.

"I can go, can't I?"

The young policeman let the question hang for a moment and air its stink of abjection.

"Drive carefully, Professor."

And so he did, cautiously negotiating the potholes in the driveway, adjusting the rearview so as to precisely center the receding provost and his policeman son. The cop had plenty of time to read his license plate, and his radio was right there, crackling ready. In another few moments, his or another cop's misery lights might well appear in the mirror, and it would all be over. Until that happened, all he could do was try to drive steadily between the headless roosters and into the night.

The Sand Car

BETTINA DIXON WASN'T expecting visitors. But then this girl—Gail, was it?—appeared, busy and blonde, with a grocery bag full of cashews and dry sherry and other goodies she somehow knew Bettina liked. After putting these treats away, the girl gazed out the kitchen window, her blunt hands resting redly on the blue Talavera tile of the counter, and said, "You live in such a healing place, Mrs. Dixon."

Bettina followed the girl's gaze to the dry, pink arroyo toasting in the September sun like an old scar.

"Yet so many people here are hurting," Gail added.

Bettina screwed a long cigarette into her silver holder. "People are hurting": that was something she'd heard the governor say on television, in conceding that New Mexico had officially become the poorest state in the Union, behind Mississippi. They weren't *being* hurt, they just "hurt," passively, intransitively. The governor pronounced it "hearting."

"I saw a man parked at the Santuario when I was driving here," said Gail. "He was lying on the hood of his car. When I drove by, he looked up at me with so much pain. Like it wants to be hatred?"

"A blue lowrider?" said Bettina. "With an airbrushed Virgen de Guadalupe on the hood?"

"Do you know him?"

Bettina struck her match on the wall and lit her cigarette and didn't reply. Yes, she knew who the man with the cobalt-blue lowrider was: Rudy Romero. It was difficult to tell his age, but she knew him to be in his mid-twenties, about like this girl. He was gaunt, ropy, with deep lines in his cheeks, but his large, green Picasso eyes were young and clear and delicately long lashed. Bettina had first encountered him one summer fifteen or so years ago, when he and another young Hispanic boy began playing around the rusted hulk of the old 1930s Chrysler in the arroyo, buried in sand to the top of its gangster wheel wells. They apparently didn't know, or care, that this section of the arroyo belonged to her, the crabby old lady painter, or that the old car was one of her favorite subjects for painting.

She had grabbed her aspen walking stick and strode out to the bank of the arroyo and shouted at them to get away from the car. "Adios," she yelled. The shirtless boy squatting on the roof of the hulk stared at her, his long arms hanging apelike between his legs, his green eyes round as a lemur's. "Scram!" she said. "C'mon, Rudy, let's go," the other boy told him. Rudy jumped down from the car and followed his friend, then stopped and stared at Bettina again. He picked up a handful of the arroyo's coarse sand and hurled it at her. It sprayed across the mat of dry leaves with a hiss.

She grasped the stick in a death grip—this was before the arthritis had set in—and shook it at him. "Stay, Killer!" she cried over her shoulder to an imaginary dog.

She learned from Sam Herrera, the postman, that Rudy Romero was an orphan—his parents had been killed in an auto accident on 285, a crash so violent it had been heard at the Santa Fe Opera, making the audience laugh, coming as it did at an appropriate moment in the performance, said Sam, who moonlighted at the opera as a parking attendant. Since then, Rudy had lived with a succession of relatives. He wasn't a bad boy, Sam said. Still, it was a good idea for her to collect her mail as soon as she heard his jeep pull up, because as the dicho went, an open door tempts even a saint.

Bettina's second encounter with Rudy Romero happened when he was a teenager. She had set up her easel in the arroyo to paint the old car and was daubing in the blackness of its shadow when he approached her, warily, like a hungry coyote.

"Like black, huh?"

Bettina had never gotten used to the Hispanic accent; it always seemed to her sharp, accusing.

"Yes, I like black. What I don't like is people sneaking up on me and looking over my shoulder."

"I could do that," he said. "I could paint like that."

"Oh, you could, could you?" she said. "Then why the hell don't you?"

Her hand had trembled with rage, and she lost control of her brush, sending a dark smear across the painted sand. She knew this was what people, ignorant people, said—"my kid could do that" was probably the most common thing one overheard in a museum or gallery—but it touched a nerve in her that day, because the reviews of her one-woman show at the Gallerías Santa Fe had just come out, summing her up as a competent but unoriginal realist. Her work, especially her arroyos, had become repetitive, a reviewer from a Santa Fe paper wrote, the symbolism of the old car disappearing into the sand trite; her best work, he said, had been the portraits of haunted, urban faces she had produced in New York, long before moving to New Mexico. Well, she supposed such reviews were to be expected; she had endeared herself to the Santa Fe art crowd even less than had O'Keeffe, never appearing at a gallery opening, not even for her own work, and always having something acid to say about the city she called Santa Fake.

And then here was this kid telling her he could paint as well as she. She watched him slouch away, his long arms jammed deep into his pockets, and regretted having snapped at him. She remembered what Sam Herrera had told her about him, that he was an unfortunate orphan. But then, let him learn once and for all what *she* was: a curmudgeonly recluse who had left friends and husband in New York City to come out to New Mexico and be alone. Not good with people: didn't even paint them anymore.

"It's better if you get to know them, I think," Gail said, dropping Bettina's spent match in the trash. "The Spanish people. Their families, you know, their history. That way they don't resent you so much."

"Who did you say sent you?" Bettina asked the girl sharply.

"The gallery?" said the girl. "Devon and Ellen of Gallerías Santa Fe asked me to look in on you?"

Bettina's cigarette crackled as she inhaled. Ah, the Gallerías Santa Fe. Exclusive representatives of Bettina Dixon landscapes, its brochure said. Or used to say. Its owners, Devon and Ellen, were too busy, as always, to come by in person, so they sent this girl. Nice of them to remember her at all.

The girl wrinkled her nose and waved the smoke away from her face. She reached into her shoulder bag, which Bettina identified as Guatemalan, and produced numerous little pouches of herbs and spices.

"There's a different tea for every ailment, Mrs. Dixon. This one helps reduce the craving for nicotine. And here's one for your arthritis—"

"What's that?" Bettina waved her cigarette like a wand over a brilliant yellow powder.

"That's turmeric. It's a blood warmer."

"Leave that one," she said, in the lull of a long, wet cough. "The turmeric. Okay, you're dismissed. Go!"

As soon as the girl left, Bettina poured a measure of linseed oil into a ceramic bowl and sprinkled a pinch of the turmeric into it. The powder left trails of gold as it sank, and the oil took on a deep glow. Might make a good pigment for painting, but she was wasn't much for that kind of experimentation. She kept to oils and to a limited number of subjects. The paintings depicting the old car sinking into the arroyo, numbering now more than one hundred, were the best example of her meticulous chronicling of a single event. Let others blather about their so-called "symbolism"; the fact was, no other artist she knew of had recorded so assiduously an object changing over so long a period of time.

The cannibalized old car was already there, half-buried in gravel and sand, when she moved into the adobe house in the village of Olmito thirty-five years before. She knew immediately that she would paint it. But it wasn't until that summer's first flash flood, which lodged a hillside boulder against the car and created a sandy spit from which mulleins sprouted, that she knew she must do a series of the old black hulk being slowly consumed by nature, a record of its disappearance. It became an island colonized first by mulleins and asters, then willow and Apache plume. Finally a tamarisk twisted out of the hole where its rear window had been. All that remained visible of the old car now was its rust-crazed roof, dusted pink with fallen tamarisk blooms.

She dumped the turmeric-tinted oil down the drain and went into her studio to gather charcoal and pad: she must go sketch her strange island, pooled in its black midday shadow. She checked to see if Osa's water bowl was full. She'd gotten Osa, a shaggy German shepherd mix, soon after the young Rudy Romero had given her that hostile look and thrown the sand at her. Normally Osa stayed around the house to guard it when Bettina went out to sketch or paint; Bettina wore a silent dog whistle around her neck to summon her in an emergency.

As she stepped outside her front door, Sam Herrera, the postman, his hair now as lustrously white as it had been black the first time they'd talked about Rudy, drove up in his wrong-sided jeep.

"We've had some reports of people having their Social Security checks stolen from their mailboxes, Mrs. Dixon. You should look into having your check sent electronically to your bank. Remember, an open door tempts even a saint."

"Do you have any idea who's stealing them?"

"There's a few people with monkeys on their backs around here, Mrs. Dixon."

"I like the phrase," she said airily, "but I have no idea what it means."

Sam glanced down the road in the direction from which he'd come and seemed about to explain something, but apparently changed his mind. "If you have your money sent electronically, then you wouldn't have to worry," he said.

"Then what excuse would I have to come out and talk to the good-looking postman?"

"*A la*, Mrs. Dixon."

Sam lurched away in his jeep, and Bettina shielded her eyes and peered down the road to see what he'd seen. Parked under the dusty elms at the crossing of Olmito's two narrow main roads was the white van that came every Friday from Santa Fe. She knew what it was; Sam wasn't hiding anything from her. It was the drug outreach van that dispensed clean needles and syringes, as well as condoms, to local addicts. "Survival kits," they were called. She knew what monkey on your back meant too—of course she did. Lord knows the art world had enough people with monkeys on their backs. She just wanted to hear Sam come out and honestly say it: heroin use has gone up astronomically in Rio Arriba County; Rudy Romero is an addict; watch your things around Rudy Romero.

And that silly girl Gail thinking she should "get to know" Rudy Romero. Well, she, Bettina, knew the likes of him well enough.

Before long, Rudy's cobalt-blue lowrider pulled up to the van. He stretched a sinewy arm out his window and the person in the van handed him a white paper bag. The tattoos on Rudy's forearm were just a blue blur from this distance, but she had glimpsed them up close one day when she passed by him on her way into Quintana's Grocery. He had been sitting in his car in the grocery parking lot, his door wide open, a needle in his right hand and a bottle of ink on the red velour dashboard, working on a death's head tattoo on his left forearm. She saw its finely detailed design, the eye sockets exquisitely shadowed, the grin at once pained and mocking. He had looked up at her and grinned with the same rictus as the death's head.

The blue lowrider pulled away from the white van and headed her way. She stepped behind a lilac, its leaves purpled with fall, and watched Rudy drive by. In addition to the Virgen de Guadalupe on the hood, she saw that the passenger door now sported an airbrushed image of a bare-chested, brown-skinned man raising his fist, a powerful, blocky figure in the style of the Mexican muralists.

Rudy stopped just before the low concrete bridge that crossed the arroyo. He shut off his gurgling engine and waited. A few seconds later, another car, primer gray, came over the bridge and pulled up alongside Rudy's. He and the persons in the other car exchanged something. The other car drove off, and Rudy got out of his car and descended into the arroyo.

Dammit. He was headed right into that part of the arroyo where the old car lay. *Her* part of the arroyo, where she wanted to sketch. She wondered if she shouldn't take Osa with her, or maybe not even go down there at all. But she refused to be frightened off. She pushed her sketchpad firmly up under her arm and grasped her favorite walking stick, the Mexican one carved with Aztec pictographs, and headed down.

The arroyo contained other castaway human things besides the old car, though these did not appear in her paintings. The earliest litter consisted of little piles of tin cans, deeply rusted, perhaps left by the WPA crews who built the arroyo's caged-rock gabions. Later came aluminum and plastic and the empty aerosol paint cans used to paint rune-like graffiti on the sides of the bridge. Most recent to appear were spent condoms and hypodermic needles. Now, as she made her way gingerly down the slope by the bridge, a condom appeared in front of her face, hanging from a Russian olive branch like some kind of revolting seedpod. She wondered why she hadn't complained, sent a letter to the governor, about the white van that distributed these things. Was it because she was she afraid of Rudy and his kind? She certainly was *not*, she told herself, as she stabbed her stick into the arroyo's coarse sand and proceeded forward.

She encountered him crouched on top of the old car, drawing something into his syringe from a spoon. So intent was he to his task that he didn't notice her. He raised the syringe up to the light, gave it an expert fillip, and pushed the plunger in a little. Then he lay the syringe beside his thigh and tied what looked like a strip of rubber inner tube to his left biceps, pulling it tight with his teeth. He slapped the death's head smartly, and when he found what he was looking for, he inserted the needle. He inserted it deliberately, almost lovingly. She had to turn away. When she looked again, she saw the needle fall from his arm and his head loll back in bliss, the lines in his face smoothing over like silt after a gentle rain.

Suddenly he jerked his head forward and looked right at her.

"Artist lady," he said, his words slow. "You. I can do . . . what you do."

She backed away, nearly losing her balance in the sand. Grasping willow, she pulled herself up the embankment to the bridge and came face-to-face with the airbrushed image on the side of his car. The figure of the clenched-fisted brown man swooped out of the blue background with startling power, coming right at her in a tour de force of perspective. She knew Rudy had painted it, because she'd seen him, airbrush in hand, working on it in front of a garage. It was hardly original, an ersatz Orozco, but the repoussoir was impressive. The son of a bitch had talent.

The retreat from Rudy tired her, and she lay down on her narrow bed. The sun, still high in the sky, cast a beam of clear light down the chimney of her corner fireplace, illuminating the cold hearth like a museum exhibit. Osa shuffled to the side of the bed and lay down with a long sigh. Bettina scratched her absently behind the ears and gazed up at the age-darkened vigas of her ceiling. The vigas bowed under the weight of the flat, graveled roof, and she imagined them snapping and burying her in latillas and tar paper and gravel. Across them spread a galactic spatter of dark spots from the time when, excited about the canvas she was working on, she had yanked a soaking brush from a coffee can, sending up a spray of turpentine. That had happened many years ago, in the days when she had easels set up in nearly every room, including this bedroom, and would dart feverishly from one painting to the next in a circle of endless creativity.

That was what it was like to be a true artist, she thought, punching her pillow into shape. You didn't have to be taught, you didn't need encouragement. What encouragement had she, a woman, gotten in those days? None, really. Yes, she had gone to art school, but wasn't school always a double-edged blade, existing as much to discourage as to cultivate? In the end, one cultivates oneself. If Rudy was truly an artist, he'd find his own way. Yes, he was an addict. So what? She had known her share of addicts and drunks who were fine, productive artists. If the stuff helped him dream, maybe it was even a boon to his creativity. Who was that addict and Warhol protégé whose paintings now sold in the millions? Basquiat. Of course, the drugs had finally killed him. That was the downside.

She pictured the bliss that invaded Rudy's face when he injected the heroin. It had been a long time since she'd been suffused with that kind of bliss when she painted. She was addicted to painting, but in the way they say a long-term addict is addicted, in a negative way, taking it to *not* feel ill, to feel normal. And that was truly horrible, to crave something not because it makes you feel good, but because not doing it makes you feel ill. Sketching and painting this arroyo over and over, this old car gradually filling with sand: Why did she keep doing it? Just because if she didn't, she'd feel bad?

She was weary, but she couldn't sleep. She got up, took two Benadryl, and went back to bed. Finally she slept, dreamlessly.

Thunder—the serious, hard-cracking kind—woke her. Lightning threw the shadows of wind-whipped cottonwoods against the wall. Osa shuddered under the bed. The storm cell hovered over them for an hour, two hours, the rain crashing down in a steady racket punctuated by the snapping of limbs. After it passed, the arroyo continued to roar.

In morning's first light, she assessed the damage. A large cottonwood branch had punched a hole in the side of her wood-shed, and her pots of geraniums lay on their sides, cracked. What shocked her most, though, was the way the waters of the arroyo had sliced into the bank on her side, exposing new pro-files of rock and gravel and leaving the roots of trees sticking into space. Another flood like this could take the trees out com-pletely, and then there would be nothing to stop the water from cutting smoothly right up to her studio and house.

The sky cleared and the sun slanted on the wetness. Water flowed only through the middle of the arroyo now. She made her way down into the gulch, forgetting to take her walking stick. Another shock awaited her at the old car: the boulder that had lodged against it for so many years had been torn away and now rested a good three feet to the side. The car itself was more exposed than it had been in years, with half the hood nosing up out of the sand as though wanting to take off into the sky.

She sat on a sunlit rock and stared at the old Chrysler, stunned. This was the opposite of what she had expected to happen; if anything, she had expected to find the car completely buried. Well, thank God. Imagine what the critics would have done with that scenario: the car, her favorite subject, gets bur-ied; soon after, she dies. Predictable, they would say, too neat. Like her work.

Now the car was in this curious new position. She could make a whole new set of paintings of the phenomenon, seen from every angle. Still, she was in no hurry to get to work. The rock on which she sat, a handsome rock dribbled with chert like a Pollock piece, gathered warmth from the sun, as did her arthritic hands, which the morning cold had left throbbing. She watched the remaining rivulets of water in the arroyo with their marrows of fine black basaltic sand. In less than a month, any water in the arroyo would wear a transparent skin of ice, under which it would bubble and stream in mesmerizing patterns.

A raven's skull-shattering caw woke her. It sat on a pine bough, heavy as a cat, watching her. The tree's shade touched her, and she shivered. Hunger put a hole in her middle. She tried to climb the bank of the arroyo, but the soil was slick and she slipped, muddying her leg and arm. Osa whined from the edge.

"Oh, you useless creature," Bettina said.

She heard the rumble of an engine near the bridge. It's Rudy, coming to do his business in the arroyo. She looked around desperately for another way up; she did not want to be trapped down there with him. But the vehicle continued along the road and sounded as if it had turned into her driveway. Osa bounded off. Why wasn't the beast barking?

"Mrs. Dixon, how long have you been down there? Did you fall? Are you hurt?"

It was the girl. Osa stood beside her, wagging her tail.

"In the order of your questions," Bettina replied, "not long, not really, and no. Get down here and give me a hand, why don't you?"

"It's a good thing I came out," Gail said as Bettina clutched her stout arm. "I heard it was the fifty-year flood, and I thought, I'd better go and check on Bettina Dixon, living out there by that arroyo!"

Bettina had never understood this business about fifty-year floods, hundred-year floods, two hundred. Nature didn't space its events neatly like that. Another fifty-year flood could happen tomorrow, and the thousand-year the next day.

"A storm like this at the end of September is so weird," said Gail. "The monsoon season is officially over."

"Well, then, it shouldn't rain a drop now, should it? Since it's official."

Gail insisted on staying and making tea, and Bettina let her, because the girl had brought croissants and they smelled good.

"Wow, the water ate away quite a bit of the sides," Gail said, contemplating the arroyo from the kitchen window. "Aren't you concerned about losing land?"

"The arroyo's land too. My favorite part, in fact. I haven't lost a thing. I've gained."

"That's what these friends of mine thought," said the girl. "That the arroyo behind their house was theirs. Then they find out it's considered an 'intermittent public waterway' or something. So these gang guys are, like, partying every night under their window, and there's nothing they can do about it."

"What are you saying? That my land doesn't belong to me?"

"Well, you know New Mexico. The property stuff can get weird. Especially when water's involved."

"I think I know *my* property," said Bettina. She bit into her croissant and tried to remember where she might have put a copy of her deed.

"Drive me to the courthouse," she said after a while, brushing flakes from her sleeve.

"The courthouse?"

"The county courthouse in TA. I want to see my property records."

"Tierra Amarilla? That's a long drive, Mrs. Dixon."

"I don't think you'll mind. Since you've taken it upon yourself to be interested."

The girl's powerful pickup stood so high that she had to push Bettina up into it. Bettina had never ridden in a vehicle so monstrous; it felt like the girl was going to run down everything before them. When they bore down on the bright-green catalpa leaves crushed into the blacktop, she imagined herself on the crest of floodwaters roaring over green-lichened basalt, and she took a deep, exhilarated breath.

They drove through Abiquiu and O'Keeffe country. Bettina hadn't been that way for years, and she had forgotten how spectacular it was. Still, those multicolored mesas and bleeding canyons and weird hoodoos were too gaudy, too otherworldly and Dr. Seuss–like, for her taste. O'Keeffe could have them.

Bettina preferred the subtler, more intimate hills and arroyos of her Olmito.

Bettina thought of the young hippie drifter who had befriended O'Keeffe late in her life and had inherited most of her estate. This had dismayed a lot of people, but it rather amused Bettina. She turned and gazed appraisingly at the big blonde girl at the wheel.

"You can certainly handle this thing, can't you?"

The girl laughed and revved the engine.

The town of Tierra Amarilla was as she'd remembered it from years ago: cold, muddy, dreary. Only the fresh red-chile ristras that hung from the sagging eaves of the porches, their pods still plump, gave color.

A silhouette of Zapata in a wide sombrero, a string of bullets across his chest, was stenciled in black on the side of a gray house. The slogan underneath read, Tierra o Muerte—Land or Death.

The courthouse stood stark in the middle of the village, all the more out of place for its fluted columns and arched windows. Bettina asked a clerk, a young Hispanic man, what the law said about ownership of arroyos.

"I can't give legal advice, ma'am. You'll have to speak to an attorney."

"As long as we're here," Bettina said, "we'd like to see the records pertaining to my property in Olmito. If you don't mind bestirring yourself."

The man had them sign a registry and led them to a cold basement. He plopped two dusty green accordion files onto a metal table and told the women they'd have to read them down there.

Bettina and Gail, under a buzzing fluorescent tube, leafed through the thicket of documents. The oldest were palimpsests written in Spanish, which neither of them understood, except for the name Romero, repeated throughout, and references to the Arroyo Bravo, as Bettina's arroyo was officially known. Then came an assortment of letters, in English and Spanish, apparently referring to the Spanish land grants, followed by bank-auction documents and maps from the US Forest Service. Finally there appeared what Bettina was looking for: the impeccable papers deeding her land to the Winchell family of Texas, from whom Bettina had in turn bought it in 1955.

"Satisfied?" Bettina asked Gail as they walked back to the truck.

"It sort of asks more questions than it answers, doesn't it?"

"What's that supposed to mean?"

"I mean, the whole land-grant thing's weird. You know about the Spanish land grants, right? About how crooked Anglo bankers and lawyers stole the land grants from the Hispanics? I wonder which Romeros they're referring to in the papers back there."

"There are thousands of Romeros."

"I went to this land-grant ceremony a while ago," Gail said. "Like a reenactment? They threw the dirt and everything. In the old days, the Spanish governor would grant the people the land, and then the people would go out to the land and give thanks to God and the king and toss some of the dirt around. That man in Olmito who paints the lowriders was there. He's a Romero."

"Is that right?"

They drove slowly past the Land or Death sign. Bettina recalled another famous slogan from the Mexican Revolution, "La tierra es de quien la trabaja": The land belongs to those who work it. And who had worked the land harder than she had, if being a landscape painter meant working the land, as she most certainly believed it did? No one could tell her that her immortalization of the tierra on canvas was not among its highest uses, its greatest celebration.

"Rudy Romero," Gail said. And then, "I think he has a drug problem. In fact, I'm sure of it. I know the signs. I've worked with junkies. But dope's not all he's about. I saw him the other day, painting his car. His car is beautiful, don't you think?"

"I have no idea," said Bettina. "I know nothing about painting cars."

Gail came often that fall and winter to visit Bettina, and Bettina was glad for it. The girl helped clean the debris from the storm and stacked firewood. It was a cold winter, or so it seemed to Bettina. Her arthritis pained her more than ever. She couldn't hold a brush now; she had to slip it through a rubber band wrapped around her finger. The lack of control frustrated her, and she had hardly painted at all lately. All she had managed were a few crude sketches, charcoal clutched in her fist, of her old car in its new posture.

Like a starving person who doesn't realize how hungry she is until she takes the first bites, the girl's visits made Bettina realize how lonely she was, especially now that she couldn't paint. Gone were the days when a few words with the postman and a private laugh at the governor's televised malapropisms were enough society for her. Sometimes Gail brought a bottle of sherry and she'd build a fire in Bettina's studio and they'd converse in the soft winter light that glowed evenly through the studio's north windows. Bettina used to avoid doing anything in the studio but paint, lest it become something less than a strict workplace. Now that didn't matter. Gail liked the studio, its oily fragrances and paint-spattered tools and half-finished works in their stretching frames, and Bettina liked that she liked it.

Gail had lived an interesting and adventurous life for one so young. Bettina could overlook her sillier New Age notions of health and healing, and the hippie-ditzy language she used to express them, as long as they came wrapped in intriguing tales of her "seeking." Her fearlessness was admirable: she had been from the Amazon to Alaska looking for paths to enlightenment and human contentment. What was refreshing about her was that she didn't seem to be seeking her own selfish personal happiness or enlightenment, except as a function of finding it in others. It flattered Bettina to think she was the latest in the girl's encounters with the wisdom of the world, and she held forth her thoughts on what it meant to live the creative life. Sometimes when she would describe a particular scene that had inspired her, the girl would look out the windows, imagining it, the calm northern light bathing her pensive face in such a way that for the first time in many years Bettina felt an urge to paint the human face—Gail's face—if only her gnarled hands would allow it.

One day, following a brief visit, she discovered Gail's other reason for visiting Olmito. It was a white-skied afternoon, and Gail had said she wanted to get back to Santa Fe before it snowed. Shortly after Gail left, Bettina decided to take Osa on a walk, because if it began to snow heavily, neither she nor the dog would want to leave the house.

She spotted the cobalt of Rudy's lowrider first, parked at the foot of the bridge; and then she saw the girl's monstrous umber pickup parked beside it. Two heads moved inside the lowrider. What on earth? Bettina let Osa pull her closer. Then the passenger door opened and Gail got out. "All right!" she said, and laughed. She saw Bettina, hesitated, then waved. Then she got in her gigantic truck and drove away.

Bettina turned and went home. She sat in her studio and wondered what she should do. Her first impulse was to phone Devon and Ellen at the Gallerías and tell them the girl was forbidden to ever approach her home again. But that would mean the end of the visits, and that wouldn't do. She watched a fly struggle in a drop of condensation in a high corner of the window and then slowly freeze against the white sky like a lost adventurer in the arctic wilderness.

"You really should let me give you acupuncture for that," Gail said on her next visit, observing Bettina's knuckles swollen round as marbles. "I am licensed, you know."

"I can't see swapping one kind of pain for another. Now if those needles were full of morphine, maybe I'd consider it."

"Don't even joke about that," Gail said. Then, as if she were sharing news about an old friend, she said, "By the way, did I tell you Rudy's on methadone now? And I've been supplementing that with acupuncture. He was like you at first: swap one needle for another? But he says it works. He calls it the new needle-exchange program."

So Gail really was involved with Rudy Romero. So this is what her self-styled "healing" had led to? The girl was an utter fool.

"He's really into his art now," Gail continued. "Did you know he has a garage full of sketches for this mural he wants to do? What's amazing is that he taught himself."

Bettina rubbed her knuckles against her palms.

"We could go over and see them. I'm sure he'd like that," Gail said.

"And I'm sure I wouldn't. I'm not a teacher, I'm not a critic. And if you ever bring him around here, you can be sure Osa'll send him off with blood sloshing in his shoes. You know, my postman has a saying, 'An open door tempts even a saint.' Sometimes I think you're the saint I should have never let in."

For the first time, Gail left her house looking offended. And Bettina supposed she had indeed crossed the line into real rudeness. Were she still painting, she would have shrugged the unpleasantness off, immersed herself in her work, and forgotten about it, the way she'd been able to shrug off having snapped at young Rudy that day when he said he could paint as well as she. But now, unable to paint, she obsessed on the falling-out and hoped Gail would come back soon so she could make up for it.

A long and lonely week passed before Gail returned. When she finally did come back, it was Bettina who brought Rudy up. She asked point-blank how his work was coming along.

"He's looking for a wall for his mural, but nobody'll give him one," said Gail. "He needs a big space, like the side of a building. I told him maybe he needed some exposure first. I said I'd talk to Devon and Ellen at the Gallerías; maybe they'd show some of his sketches. You know what he said, get this: he said it should be *galerías*, with one *L*. *Gallerías* means cock-fighting pits. He said when they got the name right, he'd think about it."

Bettina went to her bookshelves, blew the dust off her Spanish-English dictionary, and looked it up. He was right, a gallería was a cockfight arena. From *gallo*, rooster. Bettina and Gail laughed out loud. Bettina imagined the paintings on the walls clawing at each other, fighting for wall space. The word had a figurative meaning as well: egotism, selfishness.

"There's a good name for a gallery," said Gail. "Santa Fe Egotism."

"It does take a big ego, and a good bit of selfishness, to be an artist," Bettina said. "You do what you have to do, and to hell with everybody else. I should know."

"I didn't really mean—"

"Sure you did. And you're right. It's the same with your drug addicts. It's how do *I* feel? What about *my* needs? The only difference is that the artist gives pleasure, sometimes, to others. But that's not his goal. If others don't like it, screw 'em. To put it crudely. Anyway—I can see you're trying to steer your Rudy's addiction in a more creative direction. Good luck."

Good luck? Did she mean it, or was she being sarcastic? The girl must be asking herself the same thing. But why shouldn't she wish him well? Wish *them* well, Rudy and Gail both? If it weren't for Rudy, maybe Gail wouldn't come to Olmito as often as she did. The weather warmer now, she found herself puttering in front of the house, every so often peering down the road, hoping to see her in her earth-colored pickup, coming to her. Twice she spotted the drug-outreach van pull up and park under the elms, and each time Rudy drove up in his lowrider, took a little cup from the person inside, and drank. This was the methadone Gail had spoken of, apparently. Bettina recalled the time she had watched him sitting on the roof of the old Chrysler, preparing his fix. She could tell he enjoyed the ritual. Ritual was important with all drug taking, even in the making of a simple cup of tea. It was the art of addiction. There was nothing artful about the way he gulped down the cup of methadone: that was just medicine. She supposed his rituals now involved the careful honing of pencils, the preparation of pigments, the mixing of the powders with the oils, the delicious dabbing onto the palette—oh, she knew the feeling.

One balmy spring afternoon, a day when Bettina's hands were feeling better, as if the sap were returning to them, Gail appeared more solicitous than usual. She prepared Bettina a cup of ginger tea with honey and had her sit on the sofa, and she didn't make a face when Bettina lit her cigarette.

"Did I tell you that Galerías Santa Fe now has one *L*?" Gail said.

"Yes, you told me. Score one for Rudy Romero. What else is on your mind? Out with it."

Gail called it a "collaborative project." She said she had discussed it with Devon and Ellen, and they were interested. Of course, they wanted to know what she, Bettina, thought.

"Think about what?" Bettina cried.

"Okay. Well, Rudy has this idea. He wants to take the old car out of the arroyo. He thinks it would be neat to glue little tiny bits of gravel and sand all over it—completely cover it. A kind of sculpture. Like how he calls dope the Sand Man? Well, he wants to call it the Sand Car. Out with the Sand Man, up with the Sand Car."

Bettina felt a lightness in her head and a tingling in her hands. The girl was giving her a stroke. Then a cough started deep in her chest, and it gave her her fighting strength back.

"You've got a lot of goddamned nerve," she said.

"It wasn't my idea, Bettina. It was Rudy's. He said he was going to pull the car out anyway. He said it belonged to a great-uncle of his who got it stuck there and could never get it out. But Rudy says he can get it out with a good winch."

"A good *wench*, you mean. I should have known you two were up to something. Damn it all!"

But what Gail had said about the old car belonging to an uncle of Rudy Romero's gave her pause. Bad enough what she and the girl had discovered in Tierra Amarilla about this whole area having been a Romero land grant; now the car itself was said to have belonged to a Romero.

Sam's postal Jeep pulled up. She staggered out and asked him what he knew about her car.

"You have a car, Mrs. D? I didn't know you had a car."

"The car I've been painting! In the arroyo!"

"You've been painting your car in the arroyo?"

"Dammit, the old black Chrysler stuck in the sand. You know the one?"

"Oh, that old heap. That's Eusebio Romero's, but he's dead. He thought the arroyo was the freeway. It got stuck there and then it threw a rod when they were trying to get it out. It's never going to run now, Mrs. Dixon! Why are you painting it?"

She took her mail—two invitations to gallery openings— and drifted back into the house, feeling the ground shift under her feet like sand at the bottom of a stream.

"It's going to be such a cool show, Bettina, you'll see," said Gail. "In front of the gallery, the car, completely covered with little bits of granite and quartz. Inside, your paintings, from first to last. A collaboration, like I said. A beginning for him, and a retrospective for you. So awesome."

Bettina Dixon broke down and wept.

The following Saturday, the warmest day of the year to date, the wild irises already fat at the center and the lilac spikes drooping with bud weight, Bettina heard the rumble of Gail's truck. Gail parked on the road and walked up to the house. Someone else was in the truck, staring straight ahead. Rudy. Something large and mechanical rested in the bed of the pickup. The winch.

"Hi," said Gail. "Well, I guess we're gonna do it."

"I gathered as much."

"We've got a camera. It'll be recorded."

"Don't record it for me. I'm not sentimental."

"Oh, but you are!"

And it was true: when she heard the first scrapes of their shovels echoing softly down the arroyo, she wept again. Then